A STICKY TOFFEE CATASTROPHE

AN IVY CREEK COZY MYSTERY

RUTH BAKER

CLEANTALES PUBLISHING

Copyright © CleanTales Publishing

First published in August 2022

All characters and events in this publication, other than those clearly in the public domain, are fictitious and any resemblance to real persons, living or dead, is purely coincidental.

Copyright © CleanTales Publishing

The moral right of the author has been asserted.

All rights reserved. This book or any portion thereof may not be reproduced or used in any manner whatsoever without the express written permission of the publisher except for the use of brief quotations in a book review.

For questions and comments about this book, please contact
info@cleantales.com

ISBN: 9798847802062
Imprint: Independently Published

OTHER BOOKS IN THE IVY CREEK SERIES

Which Pie Goes with Murder?

Twinkle, Twinkle, Deadly Sprinkles

Eat Once, Die Twice

Silent Night, Unholy Bites

Waffles and Scuffles

Cookie Dough and Bruised Egos

A Sticky Toffee Catastrophe

Dough Shall Not Murder

AN IVY CREEK COZY MYSTERY

BOOK SEVEN

1

Lucy Hale taped the brightly colored flyer to the bakery's front counter, where all the customers would see it. Betsy Henderson, her newest employee, looked over Lucy's shoulder, her face wreathed in smiles.

"This is going to be so much fun!" she exclaimed, her hazel eyes shining with excitement. "I can't wait to pick out a costume!"

Lucy grinned, excited, herself. Ivy Creek was having their first annual Fairy Tale Fair, and Sweet Delights Bakery would be a vendor. All vendors were required to be in costume, and she suspected a lot of the townspeople attending would be dressing up, too.

It was exactly what Ivy Creek needed to get past the scandalous murder that had happened only months ago. Lucy suppressed a shudder, thinking of the close call she and Aunt Tricia had been subject to at the hands of Clara Davidson, the town's librarian turned murderess.

Hannah Curry came through the kitchen door, bearing a tray of freshly baked muffins. She was Lucy's star employee - a talented baker and decorator, as well as an old school chum. Hannah arranged the pastries in the display case before joining them to check out the flyer.

"So, what theme will we have for our booth?" she asked, curiously. She knew Lucy had hired a few of the college kids who worked at the theater to custom design their bakery stand.

"A Gingerbread House," Betsy announced, then glanced at Lucy sheepishly. "Joseph told me." Betsy had just recently started dating Joseph Hiller, the theater's production manager.

"Oh, how cool is that?" Hannah exclaimed. "Will we dress up as Hansel and Gretel, a witch, and a woodcutter?"

Lucy shook her head. "I thought of that, but when I went to the costume shop in town, they'd sold out of Hansel and Gretel. I think we should all just pick something we like. I'm considering going as Cinderella—I've always liked that fairy tale best."

Aunt Tricia, who had been setting up the cappuccino machine, looked over her shoulder with a sly smile. "I think you should! And Taylor should go as Prince Charming."

Taylor was the town's deputy sheriff, and an old flame of Lucy's. When Lucy had first moved back to Ivy Creek upon the tragic death of her parents, Taylor had been quite cool to her. Resentful, she supposed, that she'd left her hometown behind to become a food blogger in the city. But as time went by, and Lucy decided to stay and run her parent's bakery, he'd warmed to her considerably. Now they were fast friends again, and Lucy had recently felt the simmering attraction between them growing stronger.

"I think Taylor has his own costume planned," she told Aunt Tricia. "He said it's a surprise." Aunt Tricia raised her eyebrows, but refrained from further comment, much to Lucy's relief.

Lucy was glad Aunt Tricia approved of Taylor, but she wanted to be careful she wasn't jumping into anything too fast. The last thing she needed was any awkwardness between herself and her old flame. Taylor was just too important in her life for her to lose his friendship again.

"How about you, Aunt Tricia?" Lucy asked. "Didn't you go to the costume shop this morning?"

Her aunt smiled smugly. "I did. And I managed to snag the only Ice Queen costume they had left. I tell you, girls, you'd better rent your costumes soon. I know for a fact they've sold out of all their princess costumes. Gina told me she'd had a dozen in stock, anticipating a run on them, but they went like hotcakes."

"Oh, no." Betsy looked worried. "I better get over there tonight with Joseph."

Lucy glanced at the clock. Ten minutes until they opened. She grabbed her notebook and pen, and picked up her coffee, heading for her favorite table by the window. Customarily, the small staff had a pow-wow right before opening on Wednesday mornings.

Hannah and Aunt Tricia joined her, splitting a muffin, and settling into their chairs. Betsy, ever industrious, grabbed a rag and Windex to work on the storefront window adjacent to them while she listened.

"OK, guys..." Lucy tapped the pen on the pad. "I'm thinking we should use the opportunity of the fair to launch a new product. Any ideas?"

Hannah mused out loud. "Well, if you're planning to have samples at the fair, it has to be something that can stand the heat."

Aunt Tricia sipped her coffee. "I've always thought we should start a line of candies, but chocolate wouldn't do well outside all day."

"Candy would be a nice change... doesn't have to be chocolate," Lucy murmured, thinking.

Betsy piped up, scrubbing at a spot. "How about toffee? It's temperature stable." She turned to face Lucy, rag in hand. "And you could also crush it to use in your other products, like brownies or cookies."

Lucy smiled. "That's a great idea!" She scribbled on the pad. "We can make different varieties, too."

They spoke for a few minutes of what pastries were likely to sell best at the fair before Aunt Tricia looked at the clock. She stood and pushed her chair back in. "Show's about to start, ladies."

She and Betsy rounded the front counter, straightening the displays, and Hannah disappeared into the back room to continue the day's baking. Lucy unlocked the door, and flipped the sign to "Open", then sat back down, crunching numbers and making notes.

The bell rang just minutes later, and Mrs. White, one of their best customers, breezed in with a cheery "hello".

She stepped up to the front counter and eyed the display, pointing immediately to the key lime tartlets. "Ooo... that is just what I'm looking for! Can I have six of those, please?"

As Betsy boxed up her order, Mrs. White noticed the flyer. "Will Sweet Delights be at the Fairy Tale Fair, then?" Anticipation sparkled in her eyes, magnified behind tortoiseshell glasses.

Aunt Tricia smiled, ringing her up. "Yes, we will! Just look for the gingerbread house booth."

Mrs. White chuckled. "Oh, my, that's perfect. How ingenious!" She accepted her receipt and packaged tarts, grinning as she proclaimed, "This is going to be the event of the summer. See you all there!"

She gave Lucy a little wave as she passed through the front door. Just as she left, a shiny black Lexus pulled into the parking lot.

"Now, who could that be?" Hannah wondered out loud, and Lucy turned her head, looking out the window.

A man stepped out of the vehicle, locking it with a chirp of his key fob. He was dressed in a spotless three-piece suit and polished black dress shoes. He strode toward the bakery with an air of confidence, looking neither left nor right - a man on a mission. His hair was jet black, stylishly cut, and well-pomaded. Not a wisp of it moved out of place as he opened the door and entered the shop.

He paused, his cold, blue eyes scanning the room, taking it all in.

"Good morning. May I help you?" asked Aunt Tricia with a polite smile.

He smiled back at her, his bright white teeth a contrast to his tanned face. "May I speak to the owner, please?"

Lucy spoke up from behind him, where she still sat with her notepad.

"Hello. That would be me." She stood from the table and approached him, introducing herself with a pleasant expression. "I'm Lucy Hale. What can I do for you?" She took in his appearance, pegging him for a salesman.

His smile widened, showing perfectly even teeth. "Ms. Hale," he greeted her, inclining his head courteously. "My name is Rex Landon."

He offered his hand and Lucy accepted it, noting that his grasp was warm and strong. They shook hands as his intense gaze connected with hers. His next words took her by surprise.

"I'd like to buy your bakery."

2

Lucy's mouth dropped open in shock, but she quickly recovered, withdrawing her hand and shaking her head.

"I'm sorry, Mr...."

"Landon," the man supplied. "Rex Landon. Please call me Rex."

Lucy smiled apologetically. "Yes, well, Rex... the bakery isn't for sale."

He quirked an eyebrow. "You haven't heard my offer yet."

Lucy shook her head. "It doesn't matter. This was my parents' business, you see. I intend to keep running it for as long as I'm able."

He pursed his lips thoughtfully, rocking back on his heels. "Well, that's a shame," he said, glancing out the window at the quiet street. "I'm planning to build an office park in Ivy Creek, and I thought this would be the perfect location for a parking deck."

A parking deck?

Lucy fought to keep a pleasant smile on her face. "Well, I'm sorry to derail your vision," she said. "But I'm sure you understand. Beyond this being my family's legacy, I also spent several months remodeling recently. I just reopened this spring."

Mr. Landon looked around the bakery with a critical eye. "Yes, very nice," he said. "Seating capacity could be better, though."

Lucy frowned, irritation creeping in. "We have additional seating upstairs on the veranda. It's quite popular, actually. It overlooks the black walnut grove across the street, making for a very serene setting." She noticed the wry twist of his lips at her words.

She had a terrible thought. "Where were you planning to build the office park?"

He gave her a small, unapologetic smile. He looked just like the cat who ate the canary.

"Right across the street," he confirmed, a tad smugly, and Lucy's heart plummeted. "That little grove of trees will be the first to go."

Hannah spoke up from across the room. "The Carsons own that land," she informed him, in an icy tone. "I wouldn't count my chickens if I were you."

Rex tipped an imaginary hat in her direction. "You'd be losing your money, miss. My company is already in negotiations with the Carsons. Good day, ladies."

He turned to leave as Hannah bristled behind him, gripping the edge of the counter. Looking back over his shoulder, he caught Lucy's eye and laid a business card on the table by the door.

"Just in case you're curious to learn what your bakery is worth to me," he said. "I think you'd be pleasantly surprised."

He opened the door and left the building, pausing in front of his car window to straighten his tie. Seconds later, his car zoomed out of the lot and down Morning Glory Lane.

"Of all the nerve!" exclaimed Hannah, visibly upset. "A parking deck?"

Aunt Tricia laid a hand on the young woman's shoulder. "Whether or not Mr. Landon's company is in negotiations with the Carsons, I'd be very surprised if the zoning for this street allowed a business park *or* a parking deck."

Betsy looked worried, chewing her lip nervously. "Can't the town council decide to change zoning at a town meeting? There's one coming up."

Aunt Tricia sought to reassure her. "I think they'd have a lot of opposition from the residents. Remember, anyone is allowed to go to a town meeting and have their voice be heard."

Lucy nodded her head, agreeing, but privately resolved to attend the meeting, just to be sure.

The ladies got back to work, though a pall had been cast over their day.

Yes!

Lucy snagged the Cinderella costume from the rack, pleased that she had decided to visit the party shop on the way in to work. From the looks of the depleted inventory, she'd better nudge Hannah and Betsy to get their costumes soon, or they'd be having to make up their own.

The bright blue sky and sunny weather dispelled the worry from her mind as she drove over to the bakery. It was a new day, and she had all but convinced herself that Mr. Rex Landon would find opposition from the residents of Ivy Creek.

After all, who would want an ugly business park in their picturesque little town?

She let herself in the back, sniffing the air, redolent of apples and cinnamon. Hannah was hard at work, unloading the oven of trays filled with golden brown turnovers. Lucy tied on her apron, thinking maybe she'd take a few over to the police department today, and pick Taylor's brain about the zoning issue. Apple turnovers were his favorite.

"Good morning," she greeted Hannah, who was closing the oven door. "I stopped by the costume shop this morning and got my Cinderella costume. Did you choose one yet? Their stock is looking pretty low."

Hannah shook her head, grinning sheepishly. "I should have gone last night, but I got caught up watching a marathon of The Walking Dead. I'll go soon."

Lucy nodded, hoping Hannah wasn't waiting too late. She heard Aunt Tricia come in the front and wandered out to greet her.

"Did you get your costume, Lucy?" her aunt asked, tucking her purse under the front counter.

Lucy nodded, and Aunt Tricia smiled approvingly before changing the subject.

"On the way in, I noticed a 'For Sale' sign in front of where the old mall used to be, over on East Boulevard."

Lucy cocked her head, listening, as she made herself a caramel latte.

Aunt Tricia grinned. "That would be the perfect place for that Landon fellow's business park, don't you think? That is, if he's intent on building one. Myself, I don't think Ivy Creek really has a need for it."

Lucy sipped the sweet beverage, picturing the old lot, abandoned for years. It would suit that sort of development, without the need for cutting trees. *But would Rex Landon agree?*

"Maybe I'll give Mr. Landon a call," she told her aunt. "That really would be the easiest solution for him. Fingers crossed he listens to reason."

"Amen…" commented Aunt Tricia, turning to stock the cash register.

The bell on the door jangled as Betsy came in. One look at the young woman's face had Lucy concerned.

"Betsy? Are you OK?"

The girl nodded, but the distress on her face was plain. "I cooked dinner for Joseph last night at his place," she said, joining them behind the counter, her tone glum.

She took off her light sweater and hung it on a hook, tying on her apron. Her hazel eyes were filled with worry. "I've been there before, you know, but only for a quick visit. We usually have movie nights at my place."

"What happened?" asked Aunt Tricia, as Hannah came to stand in the kitchen doorway, joining them.

"Well… it started out fine," Betsy said. "I made him Papoutsakia, you know, the stuffed eggplant dish?"

The women all nodded. Betsy had been teaching herself some Greek recipes, which were Joseph's favorite. She had even taken over making the baklava for the bakery.

"We were almost through with dinner, and then it started. My nose was terribly itchy, and I started sneezing. I was so embarrassed, but Joseph was very nice about it. Then after dinner, we were sitting on his couch, and Yin—one of the cats—came up, wanting to sit on my lap."

The girl's eyes clouded. "I've never been around cats too much. My family always had dogs. But I like them just fine. As soon as Yin settled down, though, I started sneezing, and my throat got all scratchy."

She met Lucy's eyes, her unhappiness plain. "You know how Joseph feels about his cats, Lucy. Just like you are with Gigi."

Lucy's heart softened at the mention of her beloved white Persian.

Betsy bit her lip, continuing, "The sneezing—it didn't stop. I finally had to excuse myself and go home."

She looked at her co-workers, her hazel eyes worried.

"I hate to say it, but I think I'm allergic to cats!"

3

"Now, don't jump to conclusions," counseled Aunt Tricia. "It could be anything. Perhaps you're just getting a cold?"

Betsy shook her head. "As soon as I got into my car, it stopped. I haven't sneezed once, since!"

Lucy felt bad, seeing her obvious distress. "I agree with Aunt Tricia. Maybe there was just dust in his house. Don't fret about it."

She changed the subject to a happier one. "Did you get your costume yet, Betsy? I was over at the shop this morning and the selection is getting pretty thin. I was lucky to grab the last Cinderella costume."

"Joseph and I are meeting there after work today," Betsy assured Lucy. She sighed and looked around the shop. "Any more news on that real estate developer's plans?"

"Sort of. I intend to give him a call later," Lucy replied, filling her in on the other property for sale. As she finished, the clock struck nine, and it was time to open.

The morning was a busy one, with Lucy and Hannah baking cookies, brownies, and cupcakes, while Aunt Tricia and Betsy ran the front counter. The flow of customers was steady, and the veranda seating upstairs stayed almost full until just after lunch. Lucy dearly hoped she would be able to convince Mr. Landon to choose another location for his office park. No one would want to sit upstairs if the veranda view looked out over ugly buildings and concrete.

"When are we going to start making toffee?" inquired Hannah, as they paused to take a short break in the back room. The bakery racks surrounding them were full of freshly baked treats, and it was finally beginning to slow down out front.

Lucy glanced at the clock, considering.

"How about tomorrow? I need to pick up a few supplies in town today, and I thought I'd swing by the police department to bring Taylor some turnovers. He's been too busy to stop in, since Officer Blake is out sick with the flu. You know Taylor… he must be missing his morning sweets!"

Hannah chuckled. Taylor's sweet tooth was legendary. It was a wonder he managed to stay in shape.

"OK, sounds good," she said. "I'm going to work on decorating these cupcakes next."

Fifteen minutes later, Lucy was parking in front of Bing's Grocery. She exited her car and fished her ingredient list out of her purse, giving it a once over. They should have everything she needed right here, she noted with satisfaction.

"Ms. Hale!" an unfamiliar voice called out, and she glanced up. It was Rex Landon, coming out of the Fed Ex store next door.

He hurried over to her, and Lucy gathered her thoughts. *No time like the present... at least this would save her a phone call.*

"Mr. Landon," she greeted him. "I was going to call you this afternoon."

His teeth flashed. "Have you decided to sell, then?" He sounded confident, and Lucy prickled with irritation.

Her tone was even. "No. But I did see a perfect location for your office park, ready to go, no land development needed."

He regarded her silently as she continued. "It's on East Boulevard – perhaps you've seen it? It used to be a mall, but the buildings were torn down years ago. Now it's just asphalt parking lots. Quite large. You may not even need a parking deck if you make use of them."

He compressed his lips and offered her a thin smile. "Yes, I've seen it. It's not what I'm looking for. For one thing, it's on the wrong side of town. I want to build an office park that will tempt upscale professionals - doctors, lawyers, therapists. It's important the setting speaks of exclusivity. A quiet street lined with trees…"

"Trees that you're going to cut down!" Lucy interrupted, frowning.

He shook his head. "Not all of them. Just enough to suit my needs." He studied her face and leaned forward conspiratorially. "I've been thinking… I could sweeten the deal. On top of what I'm willing to pay for your land, I can also offer you a double suite in the new office park, at a discounted rate. You could run your business from there. Think of the upscale clientele you could gain."

Lucy stared at him. The man was insufferable, thinking he could tempt her with a shiny new location. He obviously had no concept of family tradition.

"No, thank you," she answered coolly. She walked away before she said something she regretted. *She'd just make sure she went to the next town meeting and let her objection to his plans be heard.*

Thankfully, when she came out of Bing's with her purchases, there was no sign of Mr. Landon. Lucy loaded the bags into her SUV and drove over to the police station, only five minutes away.

"Hey, Lucy!" Taylor was in the front room, and greeted her warmly, his eyes lighting on the bakery box she held. "Is that for me?"

Lucy took a deep breath, letting go of the negativity from her conversation with Mr. Landon. Just seeing Taylor's handsome face cheered her immensely.

Grinning, she teased him. "This? Oh, no. This is just something I decided to bring in so it wouldn't melt in the car."

His face fell, and she laughed. "I'm kidding! Yes, I brought these for you."

She opened the box, revealing the pastries, and was rewarded by Taylor's hum of pleasure. He wasted no time, picking up a turnover and biting into it, letting the crumbs fall into his cupped hand.

"Fantastic," he mumbled, and swallowed. "I haven't had the time to stop in. You have no idea how much I've missed this with my coffee." He looked around for his coffee cup, apparently left behind on his desk. "Do you have a minute? I wanted to talk to you about something."

At her nod, he led the way into his office.

"I had something I wanted to discuss with you, too," Lucy ventured, as he washed down the rest of the pastry with black coffee.

"You first," he said, and reached for another turnover. He listened as Lucy filled him in on her two encounters with Rex Landon, frowning as she disclosed the man's plans.

"So, you can see why I'm worried," she finished. "If he puts up that office park, I have no doubt it will negatively impact my business... especially the new veranda. My question is, do you think the zoning will allow it?"

Taylor steepled his hands thoughtfully. "As it stands, no. But you know, there's a town meeting coming up. If he can get the town council to change the zoning for your street..."

Lucy nodded unhappily. "That's what I'm afraid of." She sighed. "I guess I'll just have to make sure I'm there to oppose it and hope that people see it my way."

Taylor nodded, studying her. "I'll back you up," he offered.

Lucy's face broke into a smile. "You will?"

"Always," he said, his blue eyes connecting with hers. There was something in the way he was looking at her now that reminded Lucy of their time as a couple. So steady, and warm, and true...

"Lucy," he said softly, without breaking eye contact. "You know, I've been thinking. We've been through a lot together, haven't we?"

Lucy's heart started hammering in her chest. *He sounded so tender. Was he about to ask her out on a date?*

Her palms started to sweat. She wasn't sure getting romantically involved again was a good idea. What if it didn't work out and destroyed their friendship? She needed more time.

"We sure have!" Her tone was overly bright and cheerful as she abruptly stood up from her chair. She looked at her watch. "I really have to get back to the bakery, Taylor. I'm glad you're enjoying the turnovers. I'll catch up with you later."

Hurriedly, Lucy scooted out of his office, waving a greeting at the dispatcher returning to her desk. She rushed through the front door, taking a deep breath as it closed behind her, and stood blinking in the sunlight.

She'd better figure out how she felt about Taylor, quickly, before they were alone together again.

4

"...And then he suggested we move the bakery to his new office park. He offered to rent us a double suite... at a discounted rate, of course!" Lucy finished filling Aunt Tricia in on her conversation with Mr. Landon yesterday.

Aunt Tricia scoffed. "The man is delusional. Move Sweet Delights Bakery... this place is an Ivy Creek landmark." She shook her head, reaching for her coffee.

"Let's hope the rest of the town feels that way," Lucy said. "I really hope they're not swayed to change the zoning in the name of progress." She was viewing the upcoming town meeting with dread, even with Taylor there to back her.

Just then, Betsy came swinging in through the front door, her cheery expression dispelling the storm clouds in Lucy's head.

"Good morning!" she greeted them; her face alight with excitement. "Guess what I'm going to be for the fair?"

Aunt Tricia and Lucy smiled at her enthusiasm, a stark contrast to yesterday.

"I give up, what?" replied Lucy.

"Snow White!" Betsy announced, twirling, and laughing. Her eyes sparkled. "I was so disappointed when we got to the costume shop - all the good costumes had been rented. Joseph found a Pied Piper costume for himself, but I couldn't find anything until a woman came in, returning her Snow White costume, saying her plans had changed. I grabbed it right up, and it fits perfectly!"

"Good for you! You'll make a lovely Snow White, with your dark hair," Aunt Tricia said approvingly. She looked at Lucy. "I wonder how Hannah fared?"

They heard the rear door of the bakery open and shut as Hannah let herself into the back room.

"Speak of the devil…"

Hannah appeared in the archway behind the counter, huffing out a breath. Her face showed her exasperation. "Gina's shop has no costumes left that will work for me. I guess I waited too late."

"Oh, no," Betsy frowned. "But you have to dress up!"

"I know," Hannah looked glum. "I'm trying to think of something."

Lucy tapped her chin thoughtfully. She turned to Betsy. "Doesn't Joseph have any costumes left at the theater from past productions?"

Betsy wrinkled her brow, trying to remember. "Nothing that's a fairytale… Oh! There are some costumes left from Robin Hood."

"Maid Marion?" Aunt Tricia inquired, looking at Hannah's tall frame.

Lucy said, "I doubt that would work, since Denise Neary played Maid Marion, and she's very petite."

Hannah grinned. "Forget Maid Marion. I want to be Robin Hood!" She looked at Lucy, a gleam in her eye. "I still have my bow and arrow from senior year in high school. That will be perfect for me!"

Lucy chuckled. She'd completely forgotten about Hannah's high school sport of choice. If she remembered correctly, Hannah had excelled at archery, going on to compete in the state finals. "Well, then it's settled," she said, glancing at Betsy, who was making herself a latte.

"Betsy, maybe you should call Joseph this morning and make sure he saves that costume for Hannah. Someone else might have the same idea."

"I'll do it right now," confirmed Betsy, pulling her phone out.

Aunt Tricia cocked her head. "Is Robin Hood considered a fairy tale? Or a legend based in fact?"

Lucy waved a hand dismissively. "It's a folktale, which is close enough. I think it will be a fantastic costume."

Hannah seemed to think so, too, grinning broadly as she tied on her apron. She whistled a tune as she disappeared into the back to start work.

Lucy sighed. "Good. I'm glad we're all set on the costume front. And I talked to Zach last night. He said the booth is almost finished. He's added some twinkling lights, since the fair will run until ten P.M."

Aunt Tricia stood up, looking at the time. "I'm sure it will be lovely! Zach's very gifted at theater design."

Within a few minutes, their first customer had arrived, and Hannah and Lucy were kept busy stocking the pastry cases. When the morning rush finally seemed to wane, Lucy glanced over at Hannah, who was just finishing up some lemon meringue pies.

"As soon as you're done with that, let's try making our first batch of toffee," she suggested, watching as Hannah expertly browned the meringue swirls with a small torch.

"I'm game," Hannah replied, without looking up from her task.

Lucy assembled the ingredients on the counter next to the stove. For their first batch she planned on making plain, unadorned toffee, but had already decided they would offer chocolate-coated toffee at the bakery, as well.

Hannah joined her as Lucy melted the butter and sugar together on the stove, stirring it constantly until it came to a boil. The sugar caramelized as the mixture continued to cook over low heat, and Hannah sniffed the air appreciatively.

"Shall I prepare the pans?" she asked, and Lucy nodded, swirling the pot a few times and dipping in the candy thermometer.

A few minutes later she shut off the heat and stirred in the vanilla, pouring the golden-brown liquid candy into the sheet pans.

"It'll take about two hours until it's cool. Then we can break it apart," she told Hannah.

A STICKY TOFFEE CATASTROPHE

"And taste-test it," added Hannah. "My favorite part!"

Just then, Betsy peeked through the doorway.

"Hannah, there's a customer asking for you."

"Now who could that be?" Hannah mused out loud, untying her apron and following Betsy out into the front room.

An elderly woman stood in front of the dessert cases, clutching her tapestry-style handbag in both hands before her.

"Mrs. Carson!" Hannah greeted her warmly. "It's so nice to see you." She rounded the counter and bent to give the older woman a gentle hug.

Lucy watched from the doorway, smiling. She knew Mrs. Carson had been Hannah's babysitter all through her childhood years, and Hannah still spoke of the woman with great affection.

"Here, let's sit down," Hannah guided the frail-looking woman to a table.

"I hate to bother you at work, dear," the woman said, her voice thin and reedy. She lowered herself into a chair, shaking a little with the effort. Her blue eyes were rimmed with red, and she seemed distraught. There were bags under her eyes and her lined face drooped with sadness.

"Oh, it's no bother," Hannah assured her. "I can take a few minutes. Can I get you something to drink?" She looked worried, taking in Mrs. Carson's expression.

"No, thank you." The woman sighed, resting her hands on the table while still clutching the purse tightly. Blue veins stood out against pale skin, and Hannah was reminded of how old Mrs. Carson was now. The woman was silent, lost in thought, her expression suddenly blank.

"I came in to tell you something," she said, then hesitated, confused. Her brow furrowed. "It was important. What was it, now?" She closed her eyes, trying to remember.

"Take your time," Hannah said, her voice patient. Both Mr. and Mrs. Carson had been forgetting things lately.

"Oh, yes," the woman opened her eyes, seeming distressed once again. "I remember now."

Hannah sat rigidly waiting, praying that it wasn't bad news about either of the Carsons' health.

"Bill… Mr. Carson met with some fancy fellow from the city yesterday," Mrs. Carson disclosed, her rheumy blue gaze fixed on Hannah. "He went out again this morning, and when he came home, he told me he had signed some papers."

Her lips trembled, and her eyes filled with tears. "He sold our property to that awful man."

5

What? Hannah stared at Mrs. Carson in equal parts shock and dismay.

She glanced over, her eyes meeting Lucy's. Lucy had overheard the woman's words and was standing at the edge of the counter, looking troubled.

Hannah turned back to Mrs. Carson, not sure of what to say. The elderly woman was already so upset, and Hannah didn't want to make her feel worse.

"So quickly?" She managed to ask. "Did he have a lawyer look the contract over?"

Mrs. Carson sighed and shook her head, removing a tissue from her purse and blotting her eyes. "I had begged him to wait and run it by Bradley when he comes to visit next month. But he told me the fellow had his own lawyers present, and it was all handled professionally."

Hannah took a deep breath. Bradley was the Carson's son, in his thirties now. He'd recently moved a few towns over to take a teaching job. *If only they'd waited for him to look over the paperwork, maybe he would have convinced them not to sell.*

She patted Mrs. Carson's hand. "I think you should call Bradley today," she suggested. "Let him look over the forms." It might be too late, she thought, but she'd feel better if she knew someone was looking out for the older couples' best interests.

"I don't want to move," Mrs. Carson confessed, her thin hands twisting together. "Even to that fancy condo with all the bells and whistles. I've lived in Ivy Creek my whole life."

"What condo?" asked Hannah, bewildered.

Mrs. Carson waved her hand. "Oh, that man had all these glitzy brochures about some condos he's building after the new year. Talked Bill into buying one. Told him he'd better get on the list quick, or they'd be sold out." She lowered her voice, confessing, "I know we can't keep up with the property maintenance like we used to. That much is true. But I can't see myself in one of those modern buildings, all glass and steel. Without my fruit trees or my garden. What would I do all day?" Her eyes were sad, and Hannah's heart pained for her, wondering what had gotten into Mr. Carson.

"So... you won't be moving until the condos are built?" she asked. *Maybe there was still time.*

Mrs. Carson shook her head. "Bill says we have to leave in ninety days."

Ninety days! "But where will you go?" Hannah asked.

Mrs. Carson looked down with a sigh. "He was a bit foggy on the details... says he'll figure something out. He told me this was the only way to take advantage of the deal this city fellow was offering. Once in a lifetime chance, he told Bill."

Hannah was incensed. It sounded like Rex Landon had pulled out all the stops, putting pressure on the Carsons to make a snap decision *and* getting them to invest in his next business venture.

She stood up, noting the time. The pound cakes were due to come out of the oven soon.

"Mrs. Carson, I need to get back to work. Please, when you get home, call Bradley. Let him take a look at the papers Mr. Carson signed." She gave the woman's shoulder an affectionate squeeze, wishing there was more she could say.

"Now, why don't you just relax, and I'll get Betsy to bring you some tea and a danish, OK? I remember how much you like lemon danish."

The woman brightened at the suggestion, and she nodded, touching Hannah's arm. "What a sweet girl you are. Thank you, Hannah."

Hannah smiled at her and turned away, but the pleasant expression slipped from her face as she crossed the bakery.

She joined Lucy behind the counter, asking quietly, as they walked into the back together. "When is that town meeting? I need to go with you."

"Tomorrow evening," Lucy responded quickly, her mind racing.

There was strength in numbers. With both Taylor and Hannah backing her, maybe they could stop Mr. Landon's development plans before it was too late.

"Can we come to order, please?" Mr. Walters banged the gavel, and the murmuring of the crowd settled down.

Lucy looked around, flanked by Taylor, Hannah, and Aunt Tricia. Betsy had apologized, telling her she would have liked to come, but she'd already made plans with Joseph.

The town hall was packed. As Lucy's eyes roamed over the crowd, she wondered if they were all here because they'd heard of Mr. Landon's plans. *Did they support or oppose, the building of the office park?*

Mr. Walters addressed the crowd. "I know that a lot of you have met Mr. Rex Landon, who hopes to bring more jobs to Ivy Creek with his new business park. One of the issues we need to vote on tonight is the re-zoning of a residential district to allow that."

Mr. Landon stood suddenly from his seat near the front, turning to face the attendees. He nodded and smiled as the crowd buzzed with whispers. Lucy frowned, and she could sense Hannah simmering with anger beside her.

Mr. Walters said, "Rex, why don't you step up here and introduce yourself, tell us a little bit about your vision."

Mr. Landon picked his way through the rows of chairs and approached the podium. He cleared his throat and adjusted the mic.

"Greetings, my friends," he said, with an easy smile that spoke of confidence. "I've met several of you over the last few days and enjoyed talking with each of you. One thing that has become clear to me—the residents of Ivy Creek want more! More for their children, more for their parents, more for their spouses."

He looked out over the crowd. "Are you sick of having to travel an hour to go to a top-rated physician, or take your child to see a specialist? Maybe you wish there was a luxury spa, right here in Ivy Creek, that you could send your wife or mother to, as a treat?"

His eyes searched the room, satisfied, as a few residents nodded. He continued, his voice growing stronger. "Or maybe you've been looking over those ads you see on the internet for little procedures that will help you regain your youthful appearance, but you don't have time to travel to the big city?"

Lucy glanced around, alarmed to see how many residents seemed to be transfixed by Mr. Landon's words. She looked over at Aunt Tricia, who seemed equally worried.

"Ladies and gentlemen, it's time to bring all those services right here to Ivy Creek. My new office park will be designed to attract those professionals, and you won't have to waste hours on the road, traveling out of town."

He droned on some more, and Lucy began to feel sick, tuning his slick speech out. It saddened her to think that the townspeople were willing to give up the small-town charm of Ivy Creek for the sake of convenience. She hoped she'd be able to sway some of them.

Mr. Landon finished talking and sat down to a smattering of applause. Mr. Walters banged his gavel once again and asked if any of the residents would like to speak on the issue.

Lucy stood up, and he waved her to the front. As she stood in front of the room, she let her gaze connect with several of the people she'd known for her entire life.

"Hello, all. What Mr. Landon has neglected to mention is where this new business park will be. He's planning on bulldozing a property on Morning Glory Lane—right across the street from Sweet Delights—and cutting down all those lovely trees. He tried to buy my bakery because he thinks it would be the perfect location *for a parking deck.*"

There were a few murmurs of surprise, and Lucy nodded. "Yes, the bakery that my parents ran for decades, erased. Turned into a parking deck. I offered a solution for his new office park, and I'll tell you all, now, what I suggested. Why not use the old mall property on East Boulevard? It's just sitting empty."

Mr. Landon stood up, clearly irritated. He turned to face the room. "As I told Ms. Hale, the property on East Boulevard *will not* suit the plans I have. I'd rather build in another town if I can't be true to my vision." He sat back down and folded his arms as the crowd started to hum with nervous chatter.

Mr. Walters stepped back up, banging the gavel, and Lucy returned to her seat. "Order, please. Is there anyone else who would like to comment on this issue?"

Taylor stood up. "I agree with Lucy. There's no need to change the zoning on Morning Glory Lane. Find another location." He sat down.

Hannah and Aunt Tricia both stood.

"I agree," said Aunt Tricia. "Sweet Delights Bakery is an Ivy Creek Landmark. An office park across the way would ruin its lovely atmosphere."

Hannah opened her mouth to speak, and Lucy saw Aunt Tricia lay a restraining hand on her arm.

"I agree," said Hannah, through clenched teeth. She was rigid with anger.

Mr. Walters nodded, saying, "So noted. The town council will now take a vote. All in favor of changing the zoning to allow Mr. Landon's office park, say Aye."

The chorus of ayes resounded through the room, and Lucy winced. *This hadn't gone as she'd hoped.*

"All opposed, say Nay," Mr. Walters instructed.

There were a few nay-sayers, but the ayes clearly had it.

Lucy's hopes were crushed as Mr. Walters banged his gavel one more time. "The zoning will be changed to allow Mr. Landon's office park on Morning Glory Lane. Meeting is adjourned."

The room exploded with chatter, and Lucy stood up, her head swimming. *How could this be happening?*

Taylor grabbed her elbow, offering his support. "Let's go, ladies," he urged, his tone grim.

The foursome made their way to the door, where Mr. Landon stood off to one side, grinning and shaking hands with residents. He clapped one of the town council members on the back and laughed at something the man said.

Before Lucy knew what was happening, Hannah had made a beeline for Mr. Landon.

"You crook!" Hannah accused him; her eyes narrowed.

The chatter was silenced immediately, as all eyes turned to see. Hannah was angry and red-faced, pointing a trembling finger at the real estate developer.

"You swindled the Carsons out of their home! You took advantage of an elderly couple, getting them to sign papers without their own lawyer present, and convinced them to buy a condo that doesn't even exist yet!"

Hannah's voice rang through the hall as Lucy rushed forward to pull her away.

"You're nothing but a thief, Rex Landon!"

6

"Hannah," Lucy spoke in a low tone, grabbing her friend by the arm. "Let's just go."

She noticed a woman with curly brown hair standing next to Mr. Landon, regarding Hannah with a horrified expression. Mr. Landon looked outraged, his face turning purple. Everyone in the room was staring at them.

Taylor appeared on Hannah's left side, taking her other arm gently. "Let's go." His voice was calm but filled with quiet authority. Hannah allowed her friends to pull her away, as the silence in the hall was replaced by hushed whispers.

They walked through the doorway and out into the night air. Hannah turned, her expression contrite.

"I'm sorry," she apologized to her three friends. "I just spoke with Mrs. Carson's son this afternoon, and I'm so angry! The rezoning was the last straw. Bradley said the contract looked airtight... and Mr. Landon is only paying them about one-quarter of what the property is really worth."

Aunt Tricia sighed, laying a hand on Hannah's shoulder. "That is a shame, dear. I can see why you're upset. But if it was all done legally, there's nothing anyone can do to change it."

They walked as a group over to their cars.

"Just like the zoning," Lucy said, glumly. "All legal and above board… I guess we'll just have to live with it." She imagined an ugly office park across from the bakery and winced.

"Let's all just get a good night's sleep," Taylor advised. "Maybe with clearer heads tomorrow, we can find a solution."

They parted ways, and Lucy and Aunt Tricia rode home together, each lost in their own thoughts.

They arrived at the house they now shared, which used to belong to Lucy's parents. As they proceeded up the walkway to the lovely home, surrounded by flower gardens and old trees, Lucy felt comforted by the past. They opened the front door, and Gigi greeted them, meowing loudly, and twining around Lucy's legs.

"Yes, yes, I know. You were wondering where we were." Lucy bent to stroke the Persian's long white fur, then straightened and went to the cupboard where Gigi's treats were kept. Gigi purred as she nibbled delicately on the offering.

Aunt Tricia said goodnight, retiring to her room with a cup of tea and a book.

"Don't fret, dear," she advised Lucy, embracing her. "What will be, will be."

Lucy settled down on the couch with a cozy blanket, and Gigi joined her, curling up on her lap. As she flipped through different TV channels, not finding anything appealing, she thought of how Taylor had stood up beside her, backing her at the town meeting. Her mind drifted lazily between past and present, and her eyelids grew heavy. Giving up on TV, she toddled off to bed, with Gigi following closely behind.

THE NEW DAY dawned bright and beautiful, and Lucy was determined to keep things on a cheery note. Whatever the future held, there was no sense worrying about it. Hannah, also, seemed to want to put last night's events behind them. She and Lucy chatted while they baked, stocking up on the items they planned to sell at the fair.

"OK, I have to admit," Hannah said with a grin. "I'm really pumped about the fair, now that I've settled on being Robin Hood."

"Did you pick up your costume from the theater yet?" Lucy asked, as she crushed toffee with her rolling pin for a new batch of cookies. Now that they were making their own toffee, she was adding it to a whole host of products. She was even toying with the idea of a toffee cheesecake.

Hannah shook her head. "Betsy said she'd bring it today. But I did dig out my bow and quiver of arrows. It's going to be an awesome costume!"

They heard the bell ring out front, and Lucy glanced at the clock. "That's probably Betsy now."

Sure enough, moments later, Betsy peeked around the corner, holding a garment bag up. "Got your Robin Hood outfit, Hannah. I'll just set it under the front counter."

Lucy studied the younger woman's face. "How did it go at Joseph's last night?"

Betsy's smile slipped a fraction. "Oh, a lot of sneezing on my part… we finally went to sit out on the back deck. I don't know what I should do…" she sighed, and seemed about to say more, when the front bell jangled again. She peeked over her shoulder.

"It's Taylor," she said, and Lucy's face brightened. She set down her rolling pin, all covered with sticky toffee bits, and quickly washed her hands.

Taylor was standing in front of the bakery case, chatting with Betsy when she came out. He smiled, but his eyes locked on Lucy's, strangely intense. She wondered if something was wrong.

"Hey, Lucy… got a minute?"

"Sure," she replied, taking off her apron. "Do you want to sit upstairs on the veranda?" *While we still can enjoy the view*, she added silently.

He nodded his head, and Lucy led the way. He seemed quieter than usual, and Lucy's imagination ran wild, fearing bad news.

Once they were seated, she waited, her eyes on his face, as he shifted in his chair, seeming to struggle with something. Finally, he reached out his hand, seeking hers. Lucy rested her hand in his warm, calloused palm, her heart beginning to race.

"Lucy…" he began, his eyes earnest. "We've been through so much together. There have been too many times in this last year when I was afraid I might have lost you, and I couldn't bear it—the idea of a world without you in it. I want us to start thinking about the future. A future with us, as a couple, again."

Lucy's chest felt tight. She cared deeply for Taylor, but she just wasn't ready to renew their romance.

He studied her face. "Do you remember how we used to be, back in high school? I miss that, Lucy. Don't you?"

Lucy chose her words carefully. "I do, Taylor. That was a wonderful time. But..." she hesitated. "I'm just not sure we can recapture the past."

Taylor sighed, looking away. His face showed his disappointment. "I thought maybe you still had feelings for me," he confessed.

Lucy felt out of her depth. "Taylor, you are *so* important to me. But I need more time. More time to figure out what's best... for both of us." She gave his hand a squeeze before withdrawing her own.

Taylor cleared his throat, nodding his head. "OK," he said, standing up. "I can give you more time." He looked at her with a half-smile. "Just don't forget about me," he teased, and Lucy shook her head, smiling back.

He looked down at his watch. "I've got to get over to the station."

Lucy stood up and they walked downstairs together. Betsy waved a small white bakery bag from where she stood at the counter. "Don't forget your pastries, Taylor!"

He grinned and accepted the sack, saying hello to Hannah and Aunt Tricia before he turned to leave. "Have a great day, ladies," he called out as he approached the door.

There was a blonde woman outside on the sidewalk, dressed in a pink top and tight-fitting jeans. She was reaching for the door handle, about to come in. Taylor opened the door for her and stepped back, allowing her to pass.

"Ma'am," he said, tipping his hat and smiling politely. The bell jangled as he left.

The woman turned to watch him as he walked to his cruiser, her frank admiration obvious. She swiveled back around with a grin, addressing Lucy and her crew.

"Hi, there! What a lovely bakery you have here." She stepped forward, introducing herself. "My name is Charlene Tipton. I just moved to Ivy Creek from St. Petersburg a few weeks ago."

Lucy came around the counter to shake the woman's hand. "Welcome, Charlene, and thank you. I'm Lucy Hale, owner of Sweet Delights." She introduced Aunt Tricia, Hannah, and Betsy, who all chimed in their own greetings.

Charlene studied the chalkboard menu and decided on an iced mocha latte and a chocolate chip muffin, to go. As Betsy prepared the order, she withdrew a business card from her slim purse, handing it to Lucy.

"Pampered Pets," Lucy read out loud, looking up with a smile. "You have a pet grooming shop?"

Charlene accepted her items from Betsy, handing over a few bills. She nodded, her green eyes sparkling. "I do. I just rented out a space on 3rd Street, right next to the comic book shop. Do you have pets?"

Lucy nodded, thinking it would be nice to bring Gigi in for a professional grooming. "Yes, I have a Persian cat. I may stop in soon, once the fair is behind us. Are you going to the Fairy Tale Fair? We'll have a booth there."

Charlene grinned. "Wouldn't miss it! I managed to grab the last princess costume from that shop in town a week ago."

She said goodbye to Lucy, waving at the ladies behind the counter as she turned to go. "Very nice to meet you all!"

She stopped at the door, turning back with a conspiratorial grin.

"I have to say, Ivy Creek sure has a fine-looking deputy! I think I'll stop by the police station next and introduce myself... just to be neighborly."

With a wink, Charlene exited the bakery, leaving Lucy staring after her, speechless.

7

"That should do it…"

Lucy and Aunt Tricia stepped back to admire their booth, stocked with Sweet Delights Bakery goods. Fair day had arrived, and they couldn't have asked for better weather. The sky was a deep azure blue, with puffy white clouds floating lazily by, and a slight breeze prevented the afternoon sun from being too hot.

"Zach did such a great job," Aunt Tricia remarked, looking over the handiwork that had transformed their booth into a gingerbread house.

On a base coat of sienna brown, there were painted white swirls at all the booth's edges to imitate piped icing. The roof was pitched in an A-frame shape, with painted-on candies resembling peppermints and gumdrops completing the illusion. "Sweet Delights" was painted in white across the front in a fanciful script.

"He certainly did," Lucy agreed, grinning at her aunt.

Aunt Tricia looked positively regal, dressed in a shimmering silver costume with ice-blue accents. She wore her gray hair twisted up atop her head, under a glittering silver crown.

Lucy, herself, was decked out as Cinderella, with a classic pale blue gown accented in white, accompanied by clear, vinyl "glass slippers".

She still didn't know what Taylor's costume would be, and scanned the fairgrounds for his broad-shouldered form, trying to catch a glimpse. She'd been a bit taken aback by Charlene's parting comment at the bakery, but later she'd reasoned with herself. Taylor was a handsome man. It was natural that he would catch the attention of a newcomer.

"Oh, look, here come Betsy and Joseph!"

Approaching the booth now, their newest employee held the hand of the dark-haired man beside her. Lucy looked at the big grin on Betsy's face, and couldn't help but smile, herself.

"What a nice-looking couple they make," murmured Aunt Tricia beside her.

The red and black costume with white puffed sleeves complimented Betsy's fair skin and dark hair, making her the perfect Snow White. Joseph looked dashing himself, wearing an olive-green Pied Piper costume and carrying the fabled flute.

They reached the booth, openly admiring Zach's handiwork, and the foursome exchanged compliments about each other's costumes.

"But where's Hannah?" asked Betsy, scanning the crowd. "Wow, I've never seen so many princesses."

Lucy chuckled. It was true. While the accessories worn by each varied slightly from each other, the blue and yellow princess costume was definitely the most popular.

"She should be here any minute," Lucy commented, glancing at her watch. "Look, there she is!" She pointed into the crowd.

Hannah stood out from the throng of people, her rangy frame clad in hunter green. The costume featured triangle-cut short sleeves on the long tunic, a feathered cap, and green tights. She wore her own soft leather boots, and carried her bow in one hand, with a quiver of arrows on her back.

"I love it!" Betsy said, clapping her hands as Hannah reached them. She touched the feathered arrows sticking out of the quiver. "Are these real?"

Hannah grinned. "Yep, I had to dig deep into my closet to find them. I hadn't seen my old archery stuff in a decade. Thanks so much, Joseph, for lending me the costume."

She surveyed the group. "Wow, you guys look great." She swiveled her head. "And the booth is fabulous! Are we all set up?"

Lucy nodded. "Yes, all we need to do now is wait for all those princesses to get hungry," she joked.

She looked at Betsy. "It's going to be a long day, so I thought we'd take shifts, just two at a time. Do you and Joseph want to wander around a bit?"

Betsy nodded eagerly, her eyes roaming the fairgrounds. She tucked her hand into the crook of Joseph's arm, and they strolled off to explore.

"Aunt Tricia?" Lucy asked. "Hannah and I can take the first shift if you want to relax." Her aunt was getting on in years, but was stubborn about slowing down.

Aunt Tricia tipped her head, considering the packed fairgrounds. "I'll just relax in a chair in the shade here, behind the booth," she decided. "It's a tad too busy for me out there."

Little by little, customers began to stop by the booth, many in costume, with only a few exceptions. Lucy was encouraged by the enthusiasm about their newest product, toffee candy. She checked the small packages from time to time, making sure the heat from the sun didn't start to render it too sticky.

She bent to hand a cupcake to a little girl dressed as Rapunzel, with a long braid of gold trailing down her back. When Lucy looked up again, it was straight into the familiar blue eyes of Taylor. She smiled, her eyes traveling over his costume from head to toe. Her cheeks pinked as she realized he was dressed as her counterpart.

"Why, hello, Prince Charming," she greeted him with a chuckle. She cast a sideways glance at Aunt Tricia, who wore a sly smile. "Is this a happy coincidence, or did someone tip you off to my costume?"

Taylor laughed, executing a bow that was charming, indeed. "It's possible I was given a tiny hint," he admitted, then leaned closer, lowering his voice. "And I know you, Lucy. I know what your favorite fairy tale is."

Taylor's costume consisted of a royal jacket in a powder blue shade that matched Lucy's gown, embellished with a golden sash and gold military-style buttons. His slacks were white with a gold stripe and were tucked into tall black boots.

Aunt Tricia spoke up from behind Lucy. "Oh, you two look lovely! I must get a picture."

Lucy rolled her eyes, looking at Taylor apologetically. His eyes were twinkling as he held out his hand. "My lady?"

Lucy acquiesced with a laugh, coming out from behind the booth. She posed beside him as Aunt Tricia snapped a few photos on her phone.

Picture taking finished, Lucy scooted back behind the stand to grab Taylor a cookie. Aunt Tricia looked over at Hannah, who was craning her neck to look at an exhibit a few booths away.

"Hannah, why don't you take a break?" Aunt Tricia suggested. "I'll take a turn behind the counter."

"OK, thanks," Hannah said with a smile. She came around the booth, complimenting Taylor as she passed. "Awesome costume!"

As she turned away, her quiver bumped the woman beside her, dressed as a princess, with a three-quarter carnival mask covering her face. "Oh, I'm so sorry!"

"No worries," said the woman cheerfully. She stepped up to the booth to peruse the display of sweets.

Hannah hesitated, then turned back, removing the quiver. She set it down with her bow a few yards behind the booth. "I'll be back in twenty minutes," she called out, heading into the crowd.

A couple dressed as Jack and Jill stepped up next, and Aunt Tricia assisted them, answering their questions about the different brownie choices.

Taylor bit into his cookie and gave Lucy a thumbs up. "I need to be going, too," he said. He offered her a smart salute. "Thanks, Lucy."

He strolled away, and Lucy heard the princess sigh dreamily behind her mask. Lucy looked at her curiously, not recognizing the woman until she grinned. Her laughing green eyes gave her away. It was Charlene Tipton.

"That man is a hunk!" she declared, after Lucy greeted her. She looked questioningly at Lucy. "You seem like old friends. Is he married?"

Lucy was tongue tied. *What should she say? Should she lay a claim to Taylor?* Honesty won out, and she shook her head. "Nope."

She was saved from further conversation when one of the few people in street clothes approached the booth. Lucy's eyes narrowed as the man came closer, and she silently blessed the fact that Hannah was on break.

Rex Landon strode up with a sharp nod of acknowledgement to the ladies.

He looked around with a scowl. "Where's that employee of yours?"

Lucy bristled. "Hannah? Why is that any of your concern?"

His tone was bitter as he answered with a stern warning. "I'll tell you why. She had better watch her mouth, or my lawyers will slap her with a slander suit. You can't go around making public accusations like she did at the town meeting, not without consequences. She's lucky I'm a generous man."

Charlene's laugh tinkled merrily, and both Lucy and Mr. Landon turned to look at her.

"Oh, don't mind me," she said, waving a hand. "I just thought of something amusing." She turned to Aunt Tricia, who was now free. "May I have a package of that toffee, please?"

Lucy looked back at Mr. Landon, ready to defend her friend, but he was staring at Charlene with a strange look on his face.

"Excuse me," he said, his rant about Hannah apparently forgotten. "Do I know you from somewhere?"

Charlene tossed him a quick look over her shoulder. "No, I'm positive you don't."

She accepted her package from Aunt Tricia and turned to brush past him, her green eyes cold. "I'm new in town, just moved here from St. Paul."

Giving Lucy a wave, she disappeared into the crowd.

8

St. Paul? Lucy stared after Charlene, and then shook her head. She'd thought Charlene was from St. Petersburg. She must have misremembered.

Just then, another princess emerged from the crowd. Dressed in the popular blue and yellow costume, this woman had a tiara on her head, and rows of sparkling bracelets adorning her arms. She hurried over to Mr. Landon with a half-eaten ice cream cone in her hand, followed closely by a man dressed as the Big Bad Wolf.

"Rex! There you are!" she exclaimed. "We were looking all over for you."

Mr. Landon turned to regard her; his expression irritated as he focused on the woman's melting cone.

"For heaven's sake, Tina! You're going to get all sticky."

The woman visibly cringed at his tone and looked around, searching for a trashcan.

The man in the wolf costume stepped up, saying, "Here, Tina, I'll dispose of it for you." His voice was gentle, and she relinquished the messy treat with a grateful look. He disappeared into the crowd, heading for a wastebasket.

Lucy had hoped Mr. Landon would be on his way now, but both he and Tina, whom Lucy suspected was his wife, seemed content to stand in front of Sweet Delights' booth and people-watch. Lucy scanned the crowd, watching anxiously for Hannah's return.

Out of the corner of her eye, she saw a dark-haired man stride purposefully forward, making a beeline for Mr. Landon.

"You're Rex Landon, right?" The man's tone was harsh and resentful. Red-faced with anger, he stood aggressively, his fists clenched at his sides. He appeared to be in his thirties.

Rex looked at the man cautiously. "Yes, I am. Who are you?"

The man jutted his chin forward. "I'll tell you who I am! The son of the couple you just pressured to sign away their home!"

It was Bradley Carson, Lucy realized. She looked around for Taylor, a little nervous. Bradley seemed extremely angry.

Mr. Landon stiffened at the accusation, and his expression turned icy. "Talk to my lawyers," he suggested stonily. "I'm not going to discuss a perfectly legal transaction with you, here at a town celebration."

Bradley's eyes flashed with anger, and he took a menacing step forward.

"Hey now, what's going on here?"

A STICKY TOFFEE CATASTROPHE

Lucy was relieved to hear the voice of one of Ivy Creek's policemen, Officer Frye, approaching from behind the booth.

Bradley swiveled around. "This man practically stole my parents' property right out from under them!"

Mr. Landon bristled, and Officer Frye stepped forward, laying a hand on Bradley's shoulder. "Now, Bradley... you know this isn't the right place to settle something like that. You'll have to hire a lawyer and take Mr. Landon here to court, if you think something wasn't right about the-"

Bradley looked incredulous. *"If I think something wasn't right?* Have you talked to my Mom and Pop lately, Tom? They're getting on in years, you know that. They should have had legal counsel for a big decision like that. This guy took advantage of them!"

Officer Frye spoke quietly, and Lucy could barely hear him. "Son, making a public scene isn't going to get you anywhere. I'll have to ask you to move along. Take it to the courts."

Bradley shook his head, disgusted. He started to turn away, then swiveled on his heel, spitting on the ground in front of Mr. Landon.

"You'll get what's coming to you," he promised quietly, before walking away.

Rex and Tina stared after him, nonplussed. After a minute, she tugged his sleeve, whispering, and they walked back into the crowd, in the opposite direction of Bradley.

"Wow," Lucy turned to look at Aunt Tricia, who stood at her elbow, having watched the drama play out.

Aunt Tricia raised her eyebrows. "It looks like Mr. Landon has made another enemy."

Before Lucy could add her thoughts, she heard Hannah's voice call out as she approached.

"Hey, I just passed Bradley Carson, and he was so upset he didn't even see me!"

Lucy filled her in on what had just transpired, and Hannah's face darkened.

"I can't say I blame him for being upset. I'm glad I didn't have to deal with that shyster, Mr. Landon. I wasn't even aware he was here."

Aunt Tricia commented, "I read on the schedule that he'll be addressing the town later. More of his plans to be revealed, I guess."

Lucy's shoulders slumped. She didn't want to be reminded of Mr. Landon's office park, but there looked to be no way to avoid it.

The afternoon went by swiftly, with Taylor popping back by a few times, and Betsy returning with a stuffed bear Joseph had won for her. Hannah manned the booth together with Lucy for a few hours, but, just after dark, Aunt Tricia and Betsy took over, shooing Hannah and Lucy away to relax and have fun.

They had wandered around for only a few minutes, admiring the twinkling lights on the booths, when an announcement was made over the PA system, saying the musical entertainment was about to begin.

"Want to head over to the bandstand?" asked Hannah. "I heard a local band will be playing."

"Sure," said Lucy, nibbling on some fried dough.

A STICKY TOFFEE CATASTROPHE

Together they wound their way through the crowd, and Lucy wished she'd thought to bring a flashlight. Although most of the booths were decorated with lights, there was a stretch of shadowy field between the vendors and the brightly lit stage. The path was well-trampled, however, so they made their way across without mishap.

Lucy and Hannah chose a spot on the slight hill above the stage, close enough to see clearly. Within a few minutes, the crowd had settled in, with some people sitting on blankets near them, and others standing directly in front of the stage. The stars were out, and the sky looked beautiful. Lucy leaned back in the grass, gazing upward, trying to loosen the knots in her neck. *It had been a long day.*

Feedback from the microphone gained her attention, and she sat back up just as the mayor of Ivy Creek greeted the crowd. Mayor Yeats was well-liked, and the citizens of Ivy Creek applauded and whistled when he asked if everyone was having a good time.

"Well, that seems to be a yes!" he chuckled. "I'm pleased to say the first Fairy Tale Fair of Ivy Creek has been a success. Now, I know you're excited about the Primrose Band, coming up in just a minute…" More applause. "But first, I'm going to turn the mic over to a man who has some big plans for our little town. Everyone, say hello to Mr. Rex Landon!"

"Oh, brother," muttered Hannah.

"Do you want to go back to the booth?" asked Lucy. She knew Hannah didn't want to hear another word from Mr. Landon, and she'd rather not be reminded of his plans, either.

"No…" sighed Hannah. "I want to hear Primrose do at least one song before we head back. Let's wait him out."

Lucy nodded and narrowed her eyes as the real estate developer stepped up to the microphone. He seemed to be in good spirits, she thought, despite his earlier confrontation with Bradley. She and Hannah were close enough to see the man's confident, toothy smile, and Lucy's stomach churned, thinking of the destruction he intended for Morning Glory Lane.

"Hello, people of Ivy Creek!" Rex's voice boomed over the mic. "I'm so glad to be here, and to be part of your celebration. You folks sure know how to throw a party!"

Some laughter from the crowd, and he continued. "I'm not sure if all of you have heard yet about the opportunity I'll be bringing to your town, so I just wanted to say a few words about my vision. I will be building an upscale business park that will bring necessary, as well as luxury, services right to your doorstep! Does that sound good to all of you?"

His question was met with more cheering, and Lucy heard Hannah mutter something under her breath as the man continued his speech.

"That's right! My plan is all about making your life easier. No more traveling an hour or more to–"

Suddenly the lights and sound cut out simultaneously, leaving the stage and surrounding area black and silent. The shadowy figures of the crowd stirred, chattering, as people looked around, waiting.

"What the heck happened?" Hannah asked, her face just a silhouette in the darkness.

Lucy swiveled her head but didn't see any lights at all working on this side of the field.

"It must be the generator," she said. "I'm sure they'll get it fixed in a minute. There's usually a backup generator at big events."

They waited quietly for a few minutes, and Lucy wondered if they should just head back to the booth. Suddenly, the spotlights over the bandstand blinked once and came on, illuminating the stage. The crowd cheered, applauding the technicians who had saved the show.

A split second later, the cheers had turned to screams. Chaos erupted in the front row, as people pointed to the stage, crying out and stumbling away in horror.

Lucy peered down the hill in shock, not believing her eyes.

Rex Landon lay face-down on the stage, motionless, with a long and slim object protruding wickedly from his back.

9

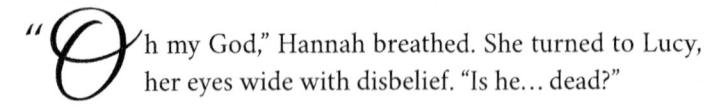

"Oh my God," Hannah breathed. She turned to Lucy, her eyes wide with disbelief. "Is he… dead?"

Several people had jumped up on the stage and were bent over Mr. Landon, trying to revive him. Shouts rang through the air as people yelled for help, and Lucy saw several officers rushing down the hill.

Lucy's mind raced. She had a very bad feeling about this. "Hannah," she whispered urgently. "Do you see what I see? In his back?"

Hannah's sudden gasp told Lucy her friend had just recognized what seemed to be the murder weapon.

"Is that…?"

"An arrow." Lucy's voice was grim. *This was not good.* She tried to remember if she'd seen any other Robin Hoods or archers at the fair.

She looked at her friend, whose face was pale beneath her freckles. "Where are your bow and quiver?"

"I left them in the grass behind our booth," Hannah whispered, her eyes riveted on the scene. She turned her head and her troubled gaze connected with Lucy's. "What should we do?"

Lucy was torn. Her impulse was to go back to Sweet Delights booth immediately, but she thought it was important that Hannah stay where she was. Obviously, up here on the hill without her bow, Hannah couldn't have been the one who shot Mr. Landon.

Additional lights suddenly blazed, illuminating the area, and Lucy was relieved to see Taylor on the stage issuing orders. He stepped up to the microphone.

"I need everyone to stay calm," he said. "Please, if you could all just remain seated. I have officers patrolling through the crowd now, folks, so there's no need to panic. Just stay where you are, and an officer will be there shortly to escort you back to the main fairgrounds. I repeat, do not panic. Stay seated so the paramedics can get through."

"Is he dead?" A woman called out.

"Was he murdered?" Another shout from the front.

Taylor ignored them, turning to crouch beside Mr. Landon's body.

Lucy turned to Hannah. "Just sit tight. It'll be OK."

The additional lights now partially illuminated the hill she and Hannah were sitting on. It wasn't long before Lucy saw fingers being pointed their way.

"That's the girl who made a scene at the town hall, calling Mr. Landon a crook," called out a man seated on the grass a few yards away. More heads swiveled, and Lucy sensed Hannah tensing up beside her.

"Hey, isn't that a Robin Hood costume? Where are your bow and arrows?"

The question came from a forty-something woman sitting close by. She had turned around and was peering at Hannah suspiciously. Her comment was overheard by several people, and the crowd began to call out to the officers.

"He was killed by an arrow, wasn't he?"

"That girl right there!"

"She's the one!"

"Arrest her!"

Lucy's heart hammered as the crowd began to turn on Hannah. *This could get ugly quickly.* Looking around, she saw Taylor had left Mr. Landon's body under the watchful eyes of several officers, and he was now walking through the crowd, talking to people, apparently unaware of the trouble brewing near Lucy.

She took a deep breath, relying on her instinct, and stood up, waving her arms, and calling his name. "Taylor!"

Hannah stayed seated, hugging her knees, trying to ignore the malicious whispering around her. Lucy shouted once more, and this time Taylor heard her, scanning the throng of people until he saw her. Lucy motioned for him to come to her, hoping he would understand her urgency.

He gave her a nod and started in their direction, and she sat back down, relieved. Taylor would make sure nothing happened to Hannah.

As he reached them, Lucy grabbed Hannah's arm, pulling her friend to her feet beside her.

"Taylor," she said, "We need to get Hannah out of here! People are starting to say she was the one who–"

Taylor held up a hand to silence her, and Lucy stopped short, staring at him in surprise. It wasn't like Taylor to be so abrupt with her. He regarded Hannah, with a grim set to his mouth.

"Hannah. Did you bring real arrows to the fair as part of your costume?"

Hannah nodded, unable to speak, her eyes glued to Taylor's face.

"It was her archery set from high school," Lucy supplied, defensively. "But you can't possibly think that–"

Taylor's gaze never left Hannah's face as he interrupted Lucy's protest.

"Where are your bow and arrows now, Hannah?"

Hannah's voice shook slightly as she answered. "At the bakery booth…well, kind of behind it. The quiver is so big, and I kept bumping into people, so I took it off, like, hours ago."

Taylor studied her face silently for a moment, and Lucy bristled. *He was acting like Hannah was a suspect!*

"Taylor," Lucy said firmly. "Hannah was here with me when the lights went out."

Taylor finally met Lucy's eyes, nodding to acknowledge her words before turning to address Hannah once more.

"Hannah, I need you to take me to your bow and arrows. Now, please."

Hannah took a deep breath, trying to steady her nerves. "OK. No problem."

She led the way back towards the vendors' booths, with Lucy and Taylor following closely behind. As the trio stepped away from the bandstand area, they were no longer illuminated, and Taylor switched on his flashlight, training it on the ground ahead of the ladies.

Lucy was grateful for both the additional light and Taylor's presence behind them. *It was hard to believe, but it appeared that someone had committed murder here tonight, and the killer was still running loose.* She shivered, her goosebumps having nothing to do with the night air.

They reached the Sweet Delights Bakery stand, and Lucy saw Aunt Tricia, Betsy, and Joseph all standing in front of the booth with stricken expressions. Apparently, the news had preceded them. Lucy met Aunt Tricia's gaze, seeing her own shock mirrored in the older woman's eyes.

Taylor touched Hannah's arm, stopping her when he saw the bow and quiver lying on the grass, a short distance behind the booth.

"How many arrows did you bring, Hannah?" Taylor asked, his voice steely.

Hannah looked straight into his eyes as she answered. "Six," she said. "It was the full set."

Taylor walked over to the brown leather quiver, studying the contents with his back to them. When he straightened up and turned, his face was filled with regret.

"There are only five. Hannah, you'll have to come with me."

10

"I still can't believe it." Lucy sat at the kitchen table across from Aunt Tricia, her face in her hands. She was exhausted, but her mind was too troubled to sleep.

They were finally home now, having left the police station an hour ago. Hannah was being held for questioning, but her parents had arrived at the station, assuring Lucy that they had called a lawyer. They urged her and Aunt Tricia to go home, and Lucy had agreed once Mr. Curry promised to telephone with any news. Lucy had been concerned this horrible turn of events would be too much for Aunt Tricia, but as she watched her aunt stirring honey into her tea, she realized the older woman was calmer than she was, herself.

Aunt Tricia set a steaming mug of lemon tea in front of Lucy and took a sip of her own. She reached across the table and patted Lucy's hand.

"It will all be resolved, dear. I know it's upsetting, but the fact is, Taylor had to bring Hannah in for questioning, since there was an arrow involved. Don't forget, he also brought in

Bradley Carson, as well as detaining Mr. Landon's wife and that other fellow… Who was he, again? The one in the wolf costume?"

Lucy answered, "Vince Byers. Apparently, he was Mr. Landon's business partner." She fiddled with her teacup, still agitated. "If one of Hannah's arrows was missing, then that means someone was trying to frame her, Aunt Tricia. Who would do that?"

Aunt Tricia frowned. "We still don't know for sure that it was Hannah's arrow in the man's back."

Lucy sipped her tea, considering. She shook her head. "It had to be. Hannah said she brought six arrows, but there were only five left in the quiver when we returned."

She looked into Aunt Tricia's face searchingly. "Are you absolutely positive you don't remember seeing anyone hanging around in the area behind Sweet Delights' booth?"

She already knew the answer, as Taylor had asked Aunt Tricia the same thing.

The older woman sighed unhappily, shaking her head. "I wish Hannah had tucked her archery set inside the booth instead of laying them nearby on the grass. The fairgrounds were so crowded... I'm sure any number of people had access to them."

Lucy nodded dejectedly. "The real question is, who wanted Mr. Landon dead?"

They looked at each other for a moment and Lucy held up her hand. "I know you're going to say Bradley, but I can't believe he would frame Hannah. They've always gotten along great, and he seems like a very nice man."

Aunt Tricia looked thoughtful. "Well, I'm sure Mr. Landon has made many enemies over the years. Maybe Taylor will be able to lift a fingerprint from the arrow itself."

Lucy nodded absently, pondering. It was true that forensic science could work miracles these days. Maybe the killer's DNA had been left on the body. She tried to visualize the bandstand area as it looked before Mr. Landon had taken the stage. *Had she seen anything out of place?* It was unsettling to think that she had probably walked right by the killer and not even known.

Aunt Tricia finished her tea and rose, setting her cup in the sink.

"You'd best try to get some sleep, dear. I'm sure by morning, Hannah will be back home."

Lucy nodded, her eyelids getting heavy though her mind still spun with questions. It would do no good to stay up all night worrying. Hannah had her family there at the station, and they'd promised to call if anything happened.

Clicking her tongue at Gigi to follow, Lucy switched off the kitchen light and headed for her bedroom.

AT SEVEN A.M., Lucy's alarm clock went off simultaneously with the ringtone on her phone, befuddling her as she woke from fitful dreams. She picked up the alarm clock and held it to her ear while smacking a palm down on her phone, before fully waking and reversing the actions.

"Yes? Hello?" She hadn't even looked at the caller I.D.

"Aren't you supposed to be baking muffins right about now?"

A STICKY TOFFEE CATASTROPHE

The teasing voice of Hannah on the other end had Lucy grinning in relief.

"Oh my God! I'm so glad to hear from you! Are you home?"

Hannah answered, "Yeah... I've been home since two a.m., but I didn't want to wake you up. I'll tell you all about it at the bakery."

Lucy protested, "No, you need to rest. I can handle the baking myself."

Hannah hesitated, then answered. "To be honest, I think I'll feel better with something to do. I'm still a little shook up. But, hey, at least I'm not in jail!" She chuckled dryly.

Lucy hopped out of bed. "OK, whatever you think best. I'll be there in a half hour."

She put on a robe and went to find Aunt Tricia to tell her the good news.

Twenty-five minutes later, Lucy had just turned on the ovens to preheat when Hannah opened the back door.

"Well, that was a heck of a night!" she announced, with a wry smile at Lucy.

Aunt Tricia came rushing in from the front room, where she'd been setting up the coffee machines. She enfolded Hannah in a hug.

"You poor dear!" she exclaimed, looking her over with a concerned expression. "Are you sure you don't want to take the day off?"

Hannah shook her head. "I'd just stew in my own thoughts with nothing to do. Better to get back to my routine." She looked from Aunt Tricia to Lucy and back again. "I've got some news."

"What?"

"What is it?"

Hannah sighed; her brow furrowed. "Well, even though it *was* my arrow stuck in Mr. Landon's back… it turns out that's not what killed him."

Lucy stood speechless, waiting.

"I don't understand," said Aunt Tricia.

Hannah explained. "I was released because the medical examiner determined the arrow tip did not cause the wound that killed Mr. Landon. The arrow must have been placed there after the murder weapon was removed. I overheard the M.E. saying Mr. Landon was stabbed in the back with a very large knife. That's what killed him."

Taking in their shocked expressions, Hannah set her mouth in a grim line. "Someone tried to frame me."

11

"What did Taylor say?" Lucy asked immediately. She was sure Taylor would get to the bottom of this now that Hannah had been cleared.

"Not too much," admitted Hannah. "He checked the arrow for fingerprints, as well as the quiver, but the only ones he found were mine."

"What about Bradley Carson?" asked Aunt Tricia. "Was he still being questioned?"

Hannah nodded, adding, "Yes, but I really can't believe it was Bradley. He didn't have an alibi since his wife had left earlier with a migraine. He said he was just walking around alone near the vendors' booths at the time of the murder, but it didn't sound like he could prove it."

Lucy was quiet, pondering. Whoever it was, they must have been behind the stage when Mr. Landon was speaking, positioned so they'd have access to the generator. Also, the murderer had both a large knife as well as the arrow on their person. *How did they hide the weapons?*

"Well…" Lucy said, unable to come up with any ideas. "I guess we'll just have to trust that the police will find the killer. I'm so glad you're not a suspect anymore, Hannah!"

Hannah grinned, always clowning. "So, I guess you won't have to smuggle in a cake with a file baked into it to break me out of jail."

Lucy chuckled. "Yep, I missed my chance."

The trio began to prepare the bakery for opening, each involved in their own tasks, but Lucy couldn't stop thinking about last night. *Had she seen something that would provide a clue?*

Betsy had the day off, but called in to check on the situation, and was relieved to hear the news about Hannah.

"Do you want me to come in?" she asked Lucy. "It's no trouble."

Lucy peeked out front. There were presently only two customers browsing the pastry case, and three seated. Aunt Tricia was handling the flow of customers just fine. Thankfully, today seemed to be slower than usual.

"I think we've got it covered," she assured Betsy. "We'll see you tomorrow."

As she hung up the phone, Hannah announced they were running low on pecans and fresh lemons.

"I can run to the market, if you want," Hannah volunteered. She was checking items off her "to do" list, and Lucy saw she still had a number of tasks remaining.

"No, you keep going," she instructed, taking off her apron and hanging it on a hook. "I'll run out and be back in a jiffy."

A STICKY TOFFEE CATASTROPHE

Lucy hopped into her SUV and zipped into town. A few minutes later she was walking into Bing's Grocery, mentally running through what they would need for the next few days.

"Lucy!" A woman called her name, and Lucy turned.

It was Patty Arkin, who lived a few streets over from Lucy and Aunt Tricia. She was somewhat of a gossip, and Lucy steeled herself as the woman hurried over.

"I can't believe what I heard this morning... is it true? Did the police arrest Hannah Curry for murder?" Patty had a gleam in her eye, eager for details.

Lucy frowned and shook her head. "Absolutely not. In fact, Hannah is no longer even a suspect." She spoke firmly, but Patty was not convinced.

"How could she not be a suspect? She had a bow and arrow at the fair, and that fellow was killed with an arrow! And everyone knows she argued with him at the town hall."

Lucy bit her lip. She couldn't disclose the details she'd learned about the actual cause of death without raising Taylor's ire, but she needed to convince Patty that Hannah had been cleared of suspicion.

"Taylor determined that Hannah was not responsible, and he let her go home after hearing her statement. She was never arrested," Lucy said pointedly. "He just questioned her."

Patty narrowed her eyes skeptically, and Lucy became irritated.

"Why don't you call the police station yourself and ask?" Lucy suggested, exasperated.

Patty lifted her nose and turned away. "I may do just that," she said, obviously miffed.

She'd thought she had some juicy gossip to spread, and I've just burst her bubble, Lucy thought crossly. She got on with her task, and soon was standing in line at checkout.

As she placed her items on the belt, the cashier looked at her with curiosity. "Didn't that girl who works at your bakery get arrested for murder last night?"

Lucy blew out a breath impatiently. "No. She had to go in to give her statement to the police, but they've released her. She's not even a suspect."

The cashier shrugged, bagging her items up. "Oh. That's not what I heard…"

Lucy looked at her with eyes narrowed and said tersely, "Well, you heard wrong, then."

She collected her bags and left the market, fuming. *Did everyone in town believe Hannah committed murder? What could she do to convince them otherwise?*

She tapped the steering wheel thoughtfully as she drove down the street. Maybe she should have a talk with Taylor. If he could announce that Hannah was no longer a suspect…

That thought had her slowing down as she neared the police station. Her eyes on the parking lot, she suddenly noticed Charlene Tipton emerging from her vehicle, carrying a large pink cake box. *That was a Sweet Delights box*, Lucy realized, recognizing the pink and black color scheme. She tapped her brakes but changed her mind at the last minute. She really didn't want to deal with Ivy Creek's newest resident right now. She'd call Taylor on the phone later.

Lucy continued on her way and was soon pulling into the bakery parking lot. Grabbing her parcels, she shouldered her way through the back door, calling out a hello. As she rounded the corner, she saw Aunt Tricia and Hannah standing in the doorway to the front room, their heads together in conversation. They both looked up as she approached, wearing identical expressions of concern.

"What's up?" asked Lucy, puzzled.

Aunt Tricia met her eyes. "Charlene Tipton was just here, inquiring about Taylor's favorite pastries."

Hannah hurried to add, "We just played dumb... said we didn't know."

Aunt Tricia continued, with a wry expression. "So then, the woman just bought one of everything! She's on her way over to the station now."

Lucy nodded. "Yes, I saw her getting out of her car." She shrugged. "She's just being nice. And Taylor had a rough night." She refused to dwell on the thought of Charlene presenting Taylor with a gift of pastries.

Aunt Tricia's gaze was serious. "Lucy... if you're having any thoughts about Taylor, romantically, I think you need to stake your claim. That woman is obviously intent on pursuing him."

Lucy waved her hand, chuckling, but her laugh had a hollow ring. "I'm not worried," she assured Aunt Tricia.

Despite her words, a little voice in her head chimed in, agreeing with Aunt Tricia, and prickling doubt into Lucy's heart.

Was she going to lose Taylor to the newcomer in town?

12

Lucy jogged through the park, welcoming the fresh morning air as dawn colored the sky with pink. She hadn't been keeping to her exercise routine, but this morning she'd decided a run would do her good. As she breathed in and out rhythmically, feeling the burn in her leg muscles, her head cleared, and she knew it had been a wise decision.

Aunt Tricia's words had echoed in her mind all evening, but this morning she felt like things just had to play out. It wasn't fair for her to tell Taylor she needed more time, but then rush in to stake her claim when another woman showed interest. If she and Taylor were meant to be together, it would all work out, no matter what Charlene did.

She emerged from the park and started to jog back home. When she came to the intersection of Pine Avenue and 3rd Street, she punched the crosswalk button and jogged in place as she waited. Across the street she could see the entrance to the Pine Avenue Inn, with its red canopy emblazoned with the logo in white. As she watched, a man and woman exited in tandem, holding paper coffee cups and stopping on the sidewalk to chat.

The light changed, and Lucy jogged across the street, coming close enough to see the couple. It was Tina Landon and Vince Byers. Her eyes narrowed as she watched Vince enfold Tina in a brief, but heartfelt hug, before the couple walked on down the street. They strolled close together, their shoulders touching, and Lucy frowned. They sure looked awfully chummy. A thought niggled her brain, and she stopped jogging.

Could Mr. Landon's wife be having an affair with his business partner?

She walked slowly back home, pondering what she'd seen. It was just a hug, after all. It wasn't like she'd seen them kissing. But, on the other hand, she knew in a murder case, domestic partners were always the first suspects. *Should she mention what she'd seen to Taylor?*

When she got back to the house, Aunt Tricia had already left for the bakery. Lucy took a shower and talked to Gigi while she got dressed. The Persian was always at her most talkative in the morning, and Lucy enjoyed the way Gigi always meowed in response to whatever Lucy said. It was almost like having an actual conversation.

Twenty minutes later, Lucy was in her car, heading to the bakery. She'd decided (with Gigi's help) to wait on telling Taylor what she'd seen, since it wasn't necessarily incriminating. Instead, she'd run it by Aunt Tricia, and see what she thought.

"Hmm. That is a bit odd," Aunt Tricia commented. "But, maybe they're close friends, and he was just comforting her."

Lucy sipped her cappuccino and nodded. "I'd hate to accuse anyone over a hug. But I think I'll keep my eyes peeled."

After all, the best way to clear Hannah's name would be to find the real murderer, she thought. She'd told Aunt Tricia last night about the gossip in town, and her aunt had advised her not to tell Hannah, assuring Lucy the talk would die down eventually.

"Oh, drat," Aunt Tricia said, suddenly. "When Hannah and I locked up last night, I forgot to bring out the trash from the veranda." She started for the stairs, but Lucy stopped her.

"I'll get it, Aunt Tricia," she volunteered. She liked to step out on the veranda in the early morning before any customers filled the space… and it looked like the clock was ticking on the picturesque view the space offered. *Better enjoy it while I can,* she thought.

Upstairs, she admired the sun filtering through the grove of black walnut trees and smiled as a hummingbird stopped by one of the feeders she'd hung. *It was so lovely up here.* She wondered if the death of Mr. Landon might affect the plans for the new office park. It would probably be up to the company to decide whether to proceed or not. She fervently hoped they would decide to just move on and leave Ivy Creek untouched.

She grabbed up the bag of trash and headed back down, glancing at the clock. Hannah should be arriving shortly. Lucy continued through the kitchen and out the back door. It was another twenty feet to the dumpster set at the edge of the property, near the street behind Morning Glory Lane.

As she approached the dumpster, she frowned, seeing the lid was wide open. *Great.* The last time someone had forgotten to close the lid, raccoons had gotten in and made a mess, tearing open the trash bags and scattering garbage. She set her bag down, deciding to peek inside first. No sense trapping any of the critters inside the container, if they had, indeed, managed to get in.

She tiptoed up and cautiously peered inside, promising herself she wouldn't scream if she saw a rat. Raccoons were cute enough, with their little bandit masks, but rats... Lucy shuddered.

The dumpster's interior was, thankfully, absent of creatures, but she did see something out of place. A lone, black trash bag sat on top of all the white bags they used in Sweet Delights Bakery. The top of the black bag was twirled tightly and knotted.

Lucy regarded it with a frown, wondering why someone else would use their dumpster. She shrugged and turned to pick up her own trash bag, ready to toss it in on top.

Bag in hand, she stopped short, as her intuition warned her something was off. Setting her bag down again with a sigh, she stood on tiptoe, reaching into the container for the unfamiliar black bag. A sense of foreboding filled her, and she knew she had to open it.

"I sure hope it's nothing stinky," she grumbled, hauling the bag out and crouching on the pavement beside it. It took a minute to undo the knot, but she eventually succeeded. She opened the bag up, peering inside.

What was revealed within the folds of black plastic had Lucy reeling backward in shock, scrambling away so quickly she lost her balance. She sat down hard on the pavement, the hairs on the back of her neck prickling with horror.

Stuffed inside the trash bag was a brightly colored garment, spattered with dark maroon stains.

Blood.

13

Flashing blue lights reflected off the metal dumpster as Lucy, Aunt Tricia, and Hannah stood watching Taylor pull on a pair of latex gloves. He had laid a clear plastic tarp down beneath the black bag to catch any evidence. Lucy felt numb with shock, her mind reeling, as Taylor carefully pulled the garment from the trash bag.

It was a princess costume. The blue and yellow color scheme looked familiar, and Lucy thought it might be the same princess costume that had been so popular at the fair.

Taylor held the costume up, and an item fell from the folds of the skirt with a thunk.

A very large butcher knife, with brownish-red residue staining the blade.

Lucy felt dizzy and stumbled back a step. It was the murder weapon; she knew it in her heart. She peered over Taylor's shoulder as he carefully turned the garment over in his hands, revealing the label.

Story Time. The same brand that Gina's costume shop carried. A princess costume that had been rented out to at least a dozen Ivy Creek citizens.

But why was it in the bakery's dumpster?

Taylor fingered the costume, examining the maroon stains splattered on the front. Lucy could tell by the grim set of his mouth that he had come to the same conclusion. *Bloodstains.*

Taylor carefully returned the costume to the trash bag and folded up the clear plastic tarp around it, packaging it to preserve the evidence. Task completed, he stood and addressed Lucy first.

"Tell me once again what happened," he instructed, pulling out his notepad.

Lucy recounted the events, but when she got to the part where she had decided to take the bag from the dumpster, he stopped her, interrupting.

"Why?" he asked, with a slight frown. "Why did you decide to remove it?"

Lucy shrugged helplessly. "I don't know. It didn't belong. I just had a weird feeling about it. Like, a sixth sense."

Taylor looked skeptical. "Then why didn't you call the police? Why did you go ahead and open it?"

Aunt Tricia narrowed her eyes at Taylor. "Oh, for Pete's sake, Taylor, Lucy didn't do anything wrong!"

Taylor looked momentarily abashed, but recovered quickly, turning his questions on Hannah.

"Hannah, have you ever seen this bag before?"

Hannah shook her head, her eyes wide.

He pressed. "Were you responsible for locking up the bakery yesterday?"

Before Hannah could answer, Aunt Tricia jumped in. "We both were. Hannah and I."

Taylor kept his eyes on Hannah. "Did you take the bakery trash out yesterday?"

Hannah looked like a deer in headlights, seeing where his questions were leading. "I took the downstairs trash out before I left," she admitted, nervously. "Tricia took the veranda trash out."

Except she hadn't, thought Lucy. *Aunt Tricia had forgotten to take the veranda trash out.*

"And did you see this bag in the dumpster?" Taylor questioned. "Or anything at all unusual? Unfamiliar cars, or strangers loitering?"

Hannah closed her eyes, thinking. "No," she answered, "Nothing out of place." She looked at Taylor. "I didn't look inside the dumpster. I just tossed the trash in."

"Hannah," Lucy jumped in. "Did you leave the dumpster lid open?"

Hannah shook her head vehemently. "I know for sure I shut it. I remember what a mess those raccoons made last time."

Lucy turned to Taylor. "Maybe you could get prints off the dumpster."

Taylor looked annoyed at her suggestion. He tucked his pad away.

"Lucy, can we talk for a minute?" At Lucy's nod, he walked several feet away, and she followed.

He turned to her and spoke in a low tone. "Was there any time that Hannah could have changed costumes at the fair? You two couldn't have been together one hundred percent of the time. Did she go off to buy a drink, or–"

Lucy's anger started to boil. "How in the world are you still trying to pin this on Hannah?" She hissed, keeping her voice down with an effort. "You know it was a stab wound, under the arrow. Obviously, someone is trying to frame her!"

Taylor raised his eyebrows. "You have to admit, Lucy, it's a strange coincidence that a bloody costume and butcher's knife show up in your dumpster, after Hannah took out the trash. If this was part of a frame-up, then why not leave it out in the open? If you hadn't untied the bag, no one would be the wiser. I can see the arrow as a set-up because it was left in plain sight. This was hidden. You don't hide evidence that you're framing someone with."

Lucy's anger simmered, but her mind raced, struggling to come up with an explanation. An idea came to her.

"DNA!" she announced. "The killer was afraid their DNA might be found on the costume, but they couldn't risk having the costume in their possession. So, this way, maybe it wouldn't be found, since the trash gets picked up tomorrow, but, even if it was, leaving it at the bakery would implicate Hannah as the killer."

She persisted, though Taylor looked skeptical. "The knife, the costume, the trash bag… if you run it through your lab–"

Taylor huffed, and put his sunglasses back on, shielding his expression. "Let me remind you, Lucy, I know how to do my job. We'll run everything through the lab, and dust for fingerprints, as well. I want you and your employees to stay away from this area—my officers will put up crime scene tape."

He hesitated then, looking at Lucy over the top of his sunglasses. "Lucy, I don't want you to take this personally. I'm just doing my job. But I have to tell you, at this time, Hannah is back on my list of possible suspects. I'll be instructing her not to leave town."

Lucy looked at him, dumbfounded. *How could he not see this as what it obviously was? Someone was trying to frame Hannah!*

She finally found her voice. "I do take it personally, Taylor. I've known Hannah for ages… and so have you! You know she's not capable of murder."

He sighed. "People change, Lucy."

She frowned at him. "Apparently, they do. The Taylor I used to know would never be so easily led."

He bristled at her words, but Lucy continued, her tone icy. "And this new Taylor? He's not someone I could ever envision a future with."

"Lucy–" Taylor's voice was pained.

Lucy turned on her heel and walked away, determined to prove Hannah's innocence herself.

14

Lucy hung up the phone, exasperated, and turned to Aunt Tricia. "That was another reporter, wanting to interview me about finding the trash bag with the murder weapon."

Aunt Tricia shook her head, annoyed. "I can't believe word got around town that fast. It was just yesterday!"

Lucy rubbed at her temples, trying to stave off a headache. "The price of living in a small town, I guess. I'm so glad Hannah took the day off."

The bell jangled as Betsy arrived. She bustled in, worry lines on her pixie face. "Any news?"

Aunt Tricia and Lucy shook their heads. They were all waiting to hear from Taylor; hopeful that the killer's DNA would be found on the costume and clear Hannah's name.

Betsy tied on an apron. "Well, maybe later today. Lucy, should I start on a batch of baklava?" With Hannah off for the day, Betsy was going to assist Lucy in the kitchen.

Lucy attempted a smile, but it didn't touch her eyes. "That would be perfect, thanks."

Betsy disappeared into the back, and Aunt Tricia spoke up, her tone low. "I know you and Taylor had words yesterday, Lucy. Maybe you should give him a call."

Lucy was saved from answering as the door opened again. She glanced up, surprised to see Vince Byers and Tina Landon enter the bakery, with Tina clinging to the man's arm.

The pair approached the counter, and Aunt Tricia found her voice first.

"Good morning," she greeted the couple smoothly. "What can I get for you?"

Tina glanced at Lucy's face; her eyes filled with uncertainty.

"Hello…" she nodded at Lucy and Aunt Tricia. "Ah… I'm Tina Landon." She hesitated and looked at the man beside her.

"Vince Byers," he said, extending his hand to Aunt Tricia first, then Lucy. Both shook it perfunctorily as Lucy addressed Tina, her voice sympathetic.

"We are so sorry for your loss, Mrs. Landon."

Tina nodded, her bottom lip trembling. She again looked at Vince, seeming reluctant to take the lead.

"Ms. Hale," began Vince, his gaze solemn. "The tragedy that occurred has left the bulk of the paperwork in a half-finished state. I see in Mr. Landon's notes that he made an offer on your bakery, but I don't see a contract. Was there one in progress?"

Lucy stared at him, surprised. "No," she informed him. "I refused the offer." She was puzzled. Everyone knew how opposed she was to the office park, and Tina and Vince had been at the town meeting.

Tina cleared her throat. "Rex said he was going to double the offer," she said in a small voice. "I wasn't sure if he had… before…" She dropped her gaze, and Vince wrapped an arm around her shoulders, comforting her. Tina leaned into him, squeezing her eyes shut and sighing.

Lucy was nonplussed for a moment. Gathering herself, she addressed Vince, saying firmly. "It doesn't matter what the offer was, doubled, or tripled. I will not be selling Sweet Delights Bakery."

Aunt Tricia spoke up. "Are you saying construction will still be going forward? Even after all that's happened?" The dismay in her voice echoed the sentiment in Lucy's heart.

Vince nodded. "Yes. As saddened as I am by the tragic turn of events, there is nothing to preclude us moving forward. Plans have been made."

Tina whispered, "It's what Rex would have wanted."

Suddenly overcome with emotion, Tina hid her face in her hands, and Vince pulled her against his chest, patting her back and soothing her. They turned away together and left the bakery.

Aunt Tricia and Lucy watched through the front window as the pair stopped on the sidewalk. Vince pulled a handkerchief from his pocket and dabbed at Tina's face as if she were a child. Finished, they walked away together, with Vince's arm looped around Tina's shoulders.

"Hmm…" said Aunt Tricia, her eyes narrowing.

Lucy glanced at her. "They do seem a bit... close, don't they?"

Aunt Tricia nodded. "More than a bit." She turned to regard Lucy, and her eyes widened with her next thought. "Wasn't Tina a princess at the fair?"

Lucy tried to remember, closing her eyes, and envisioning the argument with Bradley in front of the booth. *Yes, Vince was the Big Bad Wolf, and Tina was a princess... in a blue and yellow costume.*

Her eyes popped open, and she nodded at Aunt Tricia. "Do you think–"

The phone rang, interrupting her speculation, and Lucy said, "I'll get it," intending to send any would-be reporters packing.

"Good morning. Sweet Delights Bakery," she spoke into the receiver, grabbing an order pad and pen.

"Hello. Lucy?" The woman's voice was familiar, and Lucy tried unsuccessfully to match it with a face.

"Yes, this is she. What can I do for you?" she replied automatically, her thoughts still swirling around Tina Landon and the princess costume.

"This is Mrs. White," the caller replied, and Lucy snapped back to the present.

"Good morning, Mrs. White. I hope everyone enjoyed the key lime tartlets. What can I get for you this week?"

There was silence for a moment, and when she spoke, Mrs. White sounded troubled. "I just heard from Mrs. Ferris that the police found the murder weapon on your property. Is that true?"

Lucy gritted her teeth. *Who had leaked the story?*

"Mrs. White, I can't really comment on what the police found, but yes, they did find something in our dumpster that they took away to analyze for evidence."

There was silence on the other end, and Lucy hurried to add, "I can tell you for certain it was not a Sweet Delights employee who put the item in the dumpster."

Mrs. White sighed audibly. "Oh, Lucy, I know Hannah is your friend. But I have to say, it looks plain as day to me that she's guilty. She hated that man!"

Lucy struggled to find the right words to refute the statement, but Mrs. White continued speaking, her tone firm.

"As much as I love your bakery—and you know I do—I'm afraid as long as Hannah Curry is still working there, I won't be coming into your shop anymore."

Lucy sputtered. "But Mrs. White! Hannah isn't–"

The woman interrupted her. "I'm sorry, Lucy. I just don't feel safe rubbing elbows with a murder suspect."

She hung up, and Lucy stared down at the receiver in her hand, speechless.

15

Hannah shut the oven door and set the timer on the cake layers. Turning to Lucy, she said, "If it's OK with you, I think I'll make a dozen more key lime tartlets. I wouldn't be at all surprised if Mrs. White came back in wanting more."

Lucy flashed her a smile and nodded, busying herself with a recipe conversion. She and Aunt Tricia had decided not to tell Hannah about Mrs. White's phone call yesterday. After her initial outrage had passed, Lucy had tried to let it go. Some people were quick to judgement, and there was nothing she could do about it. There was no sense in letting Hannah's feelings get hurt.

Betsy suddenly appeared in the doorway, holding out the telephone. "Taylor, for you, Lucy." Her eyes were full of hope.

Aunt Tricia came to stand beside Betsy, hands clasped, as Lucy took the receiver, meeting Hannah's eyes across the room. They were all praying the killer's DNA had been found on the bloody costume, so Hannah's name could be cleared.

"Taylor," Lucy said into the handset. "Please tell me you have good news." Her voice was carefully neutral. She was still very angry with him, but thankful he was calling with an update.

"Lucy." Taylor's tone was measured. He could have been talking to a stranger. "The lab results came in. The blood was Rex Landon's. I'm sorry to say, but his was the only DNA we found on the costume… or the knife."

"No fingerprints? Not even on the dumpster?" Lucy was crushed. She could sense the women around her slump dejectedly as the bad news hit.

"No," he answered. "Nothing."

There was a long pause, and Lucy wasn't sure what to say.

"Um, what happens now?" She finally managed. She could feel Hannah's eyes on her.

"We're still investigating," Taylor replied curtly. A heartbeat of silence. "OK, I just wanted you to know." He hung up.

Lucy hung up the phone slowly and turned. "Nothing," she repeated. "He just said they're still investigating."

Betsy's eyes flashed impatiently. "There's got to be something we can do!"

Hannah shook her head, regarding the women with a wan smile. "If Taylor can't find the evidence, it's just not there."

Lucy looked at her friend, concerned by her dejected tone. She crossed the room to stand by her, reaching out to touch her arm.

"Maybe we should be doing our own investigation. After all, it can't hurt!"

Aunt Tricia spoke up. "But what can we do that Taylor hasn't already done?"

Lucy thought for a moment. "Well… We could go through all those photos Joseph took at the fair and see if we spot anything suspicious. After all, it seems pretty certain that the killer was someone in a princess costume."

Hannah cocked her head, interested.

Aunt Tricia spoke up. "Let's not forget, Party Time opens again tomorrow, and everyone will be returning their costumes…" The costume shop was only open Thursday through Sunday.

Lucy finished the thought. "As long as the killer's costume was rented from Gina, we should be able to eliminate all the other princesses."

"But what if it wasn't?" Hannah asked with a frown. "Story Time costumes are rented in stores all over the country."

"Let's think positive, now," advised Aunt Tricia, and Hannah nodded.

Betsy announced, "I'll call Joseph right now. If he can upload the photos to the cloud, then we can all look through them. Less chance we'll miss something." She disappeared around the corner.

The bell jangled out front and Aunt Tricia went to take care of the customer.

Hannah spoke up. "I think looking at the pictures is a great idea, Lucy. Doing something, no matter what, sure beats just waiting and worrying."

Lucy nodded in complete agreement. She'd been feeling so powerless, just standing by as Hannah was framed.

All at once, a tinkling laugh from out front caught Lucy's attention, and she poked her head around the doorframe curiously.

"There you are, Lucy!"

It was Charlene Tipton. Aunt Tricia glanced up from where she was making the woman's iced coffee, meeting Lucy's gaze with a rueful expression.

"Oh, hello, Charlene." Lucy came out to stand behind the counter. She took measure of the other woman, trying to see her as a man—specifically, Taylor—might.

Charlene was very attractive, Lucy conceded. Not delicate and feminine, but trim and athletic, her sleeveless blouse showing off her tanned and toned arms. Lucy imagined pet grooming was no easy job, what with lifting dogs onto tables and into tubs. Charlene's blonde hair curled becomingly around her face, and her green eyes sparkled with mischief.

"I heard there was some excitement here the other day," commented Charlene, startling Lucy away from her scrutiny. "Is it true they found the murder weapon in your dumpster?"

Lucy hesitated, not really wanting to talk about it. She sensed movement behind her, however, and thought Hannah must be near the kitchen doorway. She needed to make it clear to Charlene that Hannah was innocent. It was important Hannah realize that Lucy would always defend her.

"Someone left a trash bag with evidence in our dumpster," she acknowledged stiffly. "But it had nothing to do with Sweet Delights Bakery."

Charlene waved a hand. "Oh, I'm sure it didn't!" She leaned forward, lowering her voice conspiratorially.

"My theory is the killer was some psycho, passing through… saw there was a fair, and couldn't resist the opportunity to wear a costume and wreak some havoc! Do you know how many serial killers are operating in the United States right now?"

She took her coffee from Aunt Tricia, continuing, "In fact, I'm sure the killer has already moved on. I mean, it would just be stupid to stick around after murdering someone!"

Aunt Tricia commented dryly, "Yes, well, apparently our police force doesn't share that opinion. Perhaps someone should suggest they widen their suspect list."

Charlene giggled with a mischievous expression. "Well, I might just do that! I have the perfect opportunity tonight to share my theory."

"Oh?" Lucy tilted her head questioningly.

Charlene nodded, only too happy to divulge her news.

"Yes. I have a dinner date with Taylor."

16

Lucy sat cross-legged on her bedroom carpet, her old high school yearbook in front of her. She couldn't shake her blue mood since Charlene's announcement that she was dating Taylor. She'd gotten through the rest of her day with forced cheerfulness, but on the inside, her heart ached. No matter what she had told Taylor in anger the day before, somewhere deep inside her soul, she'd always thought there was a chance they would reunite.

Gigi circled around her, her plumed tail caressing Lucy, as she sensed her special person's sadness. Lucy paged through the album, stopping occasionally to study long forgotten photos of friends. A wan smile came to her lips as she read the captions. *Those had been such carefree days.* She stopped as she came to a candid photo taken of herself and Taylor, huddled together in the stands at a football game. His arm was wrapped around her possessively, and they were intent on each other, shutting out the world. The caption read, *"Lovebirds Lucy Hale and Taylor Baker"*.

She sighed and shut the album, reflecting on all the times Taylor had been there for her since she'd returned to Ivy Creek. She couldn't blame him for moving on. He'd given her a chance to pursue something more than friendship, and she'd turned him down.

She scooped Gigi up, cuddling her close. It wasn't fair for her to hold a grudge. Taylor was simply doing his job with the investigation. He was too important a friend to lose.

As she opened her bureau drawer, taking out her pajamas, she decided tomorrow she would have a new attitude. She would try to be happy for Taylor, and maybe even make a friendly overture toward Charlene. If the woman was going to settle down in Ivy Creek, Lucy felt like she should do her best to welcome her. Maybe she'd bring a gift basket by Pampered Pets the next time she went into town for supplies.

As she hopped into bed and reached for the lamp, Lucy resolved to put her jealousy behind her.

―――

Hannah, Lucy, and Betsy huddled together, peering at the computer screen. Joseph had uploaded his Fairy Tale Fair pictures to the cloud, and they scrolled through the photos, looking for anything suspicious. Lucy slowed down as she came to pictures of Tina Landon and Vince Byers together at one of the food vendors. Rex was nowhere in sight, and the couple was caught in a silly pose, with Vince pretending to bite at Tina's ice cream cone.

"Isn't that–" Betsy frowned.

Hannah remarked, "They look like a couple…"

Lucy added, "And... she's in a princess costume." She scanned the next few pictures, but Rex wasn't visible. "Hmm... where were they when the lights went out, I wonder?"

Hannah said slowly, "You know, a couple could have pulled off the murder much more easily than a single person. One person to disable the generator, the other to sneak up behind Mr. Landon."

Betsy reached for a notepad and pen. "We may as well start a list." She scribbled Vince and Tina's names down.

Lucy continued to scroll through. "Look! More princesses." She examined the photo of the crowd, which captured several princesses in blue and yellow costumes. "I don't recognize any of them, do you?"

The girls shook their heads. Lucy sighed. *This was a bit frustrating.* She moved on, scrolling down.

"Wait! Look, there's Bradley." Hannah pointed out, and Lucy zoomed in. Bradley was not in costume, but the woman he was standing next to was. She wore the same blue and yellow princess costume as the others.

Lucy clicked the next photo, and the next. Bradley and the mystery woman were definitely together, shown visiting different booths. Finally, a photo revealed the woman's face, and Lucy zoomed in again.

"That's Valerie, Bradley's wife," Hannah announced, sounding surprised. She looked at Lucy. "At the police station, Bradley didn't have an alibi, because he was alone when the lights went out. His wife had gone home with a migraine early on. I didn't realize she had been in costume."

"I'm adding her to the list," Betsy announced, scribbling away.

"I wonder if Taylor knows Bradley's wife was in a princess costume…" Lucy wondered out loud. *Maybe she should call him.*

Hannah was quiet for a moment, her expression sober. "Gosh, I really hate to think of Bradley and his wife as suspects."

"Well, there are more princesses in these pictures. We just don't know who they are," Betsy pointed out.

They came next to a picture of Charlene, in her princess costume and mask. The silence was uncomfortable for a moment, as both Hannah and Betsy were sensitive to Lucy's feelings about Charlene and Taylor dating.

"Another one for the list," Lucy said, keeping her tone casual, and Betsy jotted down Charlene's name.

The bell jangled downstairs. Aunt Tricia had arrived. Lucy glanced at the clock.

"I guess that's all for now, ladies. Betsy, please tell Joseph thank you for uploading the pictures."

The women left the office and headed for the stairs. "How are things going with the cats and the sneezing?" asked Hannah.

Betsy shook her head sadly. "Terrible. Every time I go into Joseph's house, I have a sneezing fit. We've started only meeting at my place. He's being very nice about it, but obviously, I can't avoid his cats forever."

Lucy looked at the younger girl sympathetically. She knew how much Betsy cared for Joseph. "Maybe you should go to an allergist and get tested. Then, at least you'll know for sure."

Betsy sighed. "I'm afraid to find out. But you're right. I should get tested."

They reached the bottom of the steps and greeted Aunt Tricia, who was stocking the register.

"Good morning," she replied, finishing her task, and looking at Lucy questioningly. "Find anything?"

"Maybe," replied Lucy. "I'll tell you about it after the morning rush." She flipped the sign on the door to 'Open'.

There was no morning rush. For the first time in months, the bakery traffic had slowed to a trickle. Only three customers came in before noon, and none elected to stay, taking their purchases to go. Dozens of fresh baked pastries sat crowding the display cases. The veranda stayed empty.

"What is going on?" asked Betsy. "Is there a parade or something on Main Street?"

She looked truly puzzled. Lucy and Aunt Tricia exchanged glances, thinking the same thing. Lucy didn't want to say it, but she was certain the town was joining along with Mrs. White in her boycott.

Hannah approached Lucy, asking her quietly, "Can I talk to you in private?"

Lucy nodded and led the way back into the kitchen. She was afraid Hannah was going to question her and wasn't sure what she should say.

Hannah took a deep breath, looking into Lucy's eyes.

"I hate to have to say this, Lucy, but… I can't work for you anymore."

Lucy's eyes widened in shock as Hannah continued, her tone firm.

"I quit."

17

"No, Hannah," Lucy said, shaking her head. She knew where Hannah was going with this. Her friend was generous to a fault.

"I have to, Lucy. I know that the town still suspects me because of the arrow. And then, the murder weapon found in our dumpster… you know that's why everyone's avoiding Sweet Delights. I can't let my troubles damage your bakery's reputation."

Lucy took Hannah's arms, her eyes locked with hers. "*I am standing by you*. We are all standing by you. This town has shunned Sweet Delights before over a perceived scandal, and they've gotten over it, and come back. This will all go away, as soon as the killer is found."

Hannah looked miserable. "What if they don't find the killer?"

Lucy said firmly, "I have complete confidence in Taylor and in us! There's no way whoever did this is going to get away with murder."

Hannah was silent for a moment, considering Lucy's words. She looked doubtful. "You're really sweet, Lucy, but I think I should at least take a couple weeks off. Maybe they'll solve the murder by then and…"

Lucy shook her head firmly. "Hannah, if you stop working here for a couple of weeks, even if we call it a vacation, all it will do is make people think you're running away. Rumors will spread faster. People will say I didn't want you here, because *I* thought you were guilty."

Hannah looked stricken, and Lucy knew she had made a good point.

She stepped back, and pivoted, snagging Hannah's apron off the hook behind her. She turned back to face her friend and assistant.

"I need you, Hannah. You're my right hand. We should look at this like we do any slow season – a time to stock up and feed the freezer. Eventually, things will pick back up. I might even go to town and see if I can get some shops to start carrying our toffee."

She held the apron out. "Can I count on you?"

Hannah hesitated, then reached out and accepted the apron. "Always, Lucy." Without further comment, she tied on her apron and picked up her "to do" list, scanning it.

Lucy sighed inwardly, thankful to have avoided the crisis. *Sweet Delights Bakery couldn't lose Hannah!* She was determined to clear her friend's name.

She stepped out front where Aunt Tricia and Betsy were straightening displays.

"Do we have any empty baskets around, Aunt Tricia? I seem to remember seeing one, but I can't recall where."

Aunt Tricia nodded at the cupboard under the local honey display. "I think there's one in there."

Lucy crossed to the cabinet and retrieved it. "Thanks!"

"Who are you making a basket for?" Betsy asked, as Lucy began to add a few soaps and candles from Bee Natural, a local apiary's display.

"Charlene Tipton."

Both women stopped what they were doing and gaped at Lucy.

"Why would you do that?" Aunt Tricia asked, her brow wrinkled.

Lucy moved on to the local blueberry preserves they carried, adding a jar. "It's a welcome basket. I'm being a good neighbor," she said jokingly. Met with silence, she looked at their identical shocked faces.

"Listen, I don't have a claim on Taylor. Recently, he asked me if I wanted to start dating again, and I told him no. It's only natural that he would move on." Lucy added a package of toffee candy, a selection of mini pastries, and eyed her basket. She needed some ribbon.

"I'll be in my office for a few minutes," she called out as she headed for the stairs.

Upstairs, she found a spool of purple curling ribbon and tucked it into her apron pocket. She'd decorate the basket and visit Charlene's shop this afternoon.

Sitting at her desk, her thoughts turned to Hannah once again, and she considered taking another look at the photos. *There had to be a clue in there somewhere.* Betsy's list caught her eye and she picked it up.

Vince Byers and Tina Landon... Valerie Carson... Charlene Tipton.

Who had the best motive to kill Rex Landon? If his wife and business partner were indeed having an affair, they would seem the most likely suspects. Bradley Carson had a motive too... but why would his wife be the one to stab Mr. Landon? Unless Bradley knew he couldn't get close enough without alarming the man, given they'd already had an altercation. She drummed her pen on the desk, thinking about Charlene Tipton. She couldn't come up with a motive for the pet groomer to want Rex Landon dead. And it would be harder for a lone individual to both kill the generator and fatally attack the man in just a few minutes' time.

Lucy sighed and glanced at her calendar, remembering Party Time opened back up this morning. Some people may have returned their costumes on Sunday, but technically, they were all due back today. She didn't know if Gina would give her the information she needed, but she had to try. She quickly found the number for Party Time on the internet, and a few minutes later was ringing the line.

Gina answered. "Party Time. How may I help you?"

Lucy crossed her fingers. "Hey, Gina, it's Lucy." She strove to keep her voice casual.

Gina replied, "Oh, hi, Lucy." Her tone was somewhat subdued, and Lucy suspected she'd heard about the murder weapon being found in Sweet Delights' dumpster. "Um... how are you?"

Lucy decided to just lay it on the line. "I'm OK. Listen, Gina, I was hoping you'd do me a favor. Is there anyway you can verify for me if any of the princess costumes you rented for the fair are still out?"

Gina sighed. "I'm not sure if I should be telling you this, but no one asked me to keep it quiet, so I guess it's OK. Taylor called a few hours ago to ask the same question. I'm guessing this has to do with the murder. Did they really find the murder weapon in your dumpster?"

Lucy clutched the receiver tightly. "I'm not supposed to comment on that. Please, Gina, it's really important."

Gina hesitated for a second before replying. "When Taylor called, Valerie Carson still hadn't returned her princess costume."

Lucy perked up. "Really?" *Was it Valerie's bloody costume in the dumpster?*

Gina continued, "But just a half hour ago, Bradley came in and returned it."

Lucy's hope crashed. "So…"

Gina's voice came over the line, her words confirming the dead end.

"Every single princess costume has now been checked back in, Lucy."

18

"That doesn't mean anything," Aunt Tricia argued, after hearing the news. "Several of the 'princesses' came from out of town. Valerie Carson, Tina Landon, and Charlene Tipton, to name the ones we know of. There may even be others. Any of them could have rented the same princess costume at another store."

"Story Time costumes *are* nationwide," Hannah pointed out.

"And then by renting and returning another costume in Ivy Creek, they'd have an alibi!" Betsy chimed in excitedly.

Lucy realized they were right. But what should they do now? Calling all the costume shops in surrounding towns seemed like a pretty daunting task. And unlike Gina, most shop owners wouldn't be inclined to give Lucy the time of day. *But the shop owners would talk to the police...*

Lucy decided it was time to mend fences with Taylor. If she was going to be honest with herself, she knew she'd overreacted. Taylor was only doing his job, and it might be beneficial to Hannah if Lucy could share her theories with him. Besides, it was driving her crazy not knowing what progress he was making!

She looked at the clock. She was intending to drop off her welcome basket at Pampered Pets this afternoon. While she was out, she may as well bring a peace offering to Taylor.

"Time to bring out the big guns!" she announced, looking at the display case. "I'm going to stop by the police station after I deliver my basket." She started filling a bakery box with Taylor's favorite treats.

"Are you going to apologize to Taylor?" Aunt Tricia asked hopefully. She hated seeing Lucy and Taylor on the outs.

"I'm hoping I don't have to," answered Lucy truthfully. "I am going to stop by and talk to him, at least, and let him know I'm not angry."

Fifteen minutes later, Lucy was pulling up in front of Pampered Pets. As she walked up to the door, she admired the planters filled with colorful zinnias set out front on the sidewalk. Charlene had put out a handmade sign on the door, proclaiming, "All four footed and two footed creatures are welcome here!"

Lucy smiled and opened the door, stepping inside. The retail space was split primarily into two areas—cats and dogs, and there was a glassed-in space at the back with a few tables and a tub—the grooming area. She glanced at the front counter and didn't see Charlene, but she thought she could hear a person talking on the phone.

Unobtrusively, Lucy drifted through the cat area, scoping out the cat beds and condos on the far side of the store. Some had sale tags in red, and she lifted a tag, thinking Gigi might appreciate a new bed. The price was quite reasonable, and she stored the idea away for a future splurge.

As she moved on to another row, this one full of feline supplements and treats, the voice got louder. It was definitely Charlene; her tinkling laugh was a dead giveaway. Lucy stopped directly in front of a door marked "Employees Only", curious despite herself. Charlene could be heard clearly.

"I tell you what, another six weeks in this godforsaken town is about all I can stand! There's not even a decent restaurant. The whole town just rolls up the sidewalk at ten PM."

Lucy frowned. *Was Charlene planning on leaving? She'd given every indication of being here to stay.*

She moved away from the door, not wanting to be caught eavesdropping. She elected to stand in front of the counter, and set her basket down, making a point of clearing her throat loudly.

A few seconds later, Charlene emerged from the same door. Spotting Lucy, she hurried forward with a smile.

"Well, hello!" She spotted the basket and her eyes lit up. "Is that for me?"

Lucy forced a smile, though her mind raced with questions. "Yes. I wanted to properly welcome you to Ivy Creek. Sorry, it took a while."

Charlene dove into the basket with glee, holding up different items, and marveling at the soaps from Bee Natural.

"This was just so thoughtful of you, Lucy." She met Lucy's gaze. "I know you have a lot going on right now."

The meaning was obvious, but Lucy brushed it off. "How's business? I love your shop!"

Charlene nodded, looking pleased. "I can't complain. A steady flow of appointments, getting more every day. I'm hoping to run a Christmas special with holiday pet pictures included with grooming."

Lucy kept her smile in place, wondering what kind of game Charlene was playing. Her words on the telephone were so full of derision and impatience to leave Ivy Creek, yet here she was, acting as though she couldn't be happier.

Charlene glanced at the clock. "Oh, sorry, Lucy, but I've got to get ready for my next appointment. Thank you so much for the gift basket!"

Lucy said, "Oh, no worries. You're welcome." She waved goodbye, heading for the door.

She drove over to the police station, worrying over what she'd heard. Something strange was going on. Charlene's intentions seemed convoluted. Even though she knew it was dangerous territory, she felt like she had to mention it to Taylor. After all, what would happen if he lost his heart to Charlene, unaware that she hated Ivy Creek?

She opened the police station door, and was waved toward Taylor's office by the dispatcher, who was on the phone. Lucy knocked and entered when she heard his familiar voice.

"Hi, Taylor," she greeted him, her eyes running over him. He looked tired, she thought. This investigation wasn't easy on him, either.

"Lucy." He sounded surprised, and just a little bit pleased. It was that nuance in his tone that had her offering him a sweet smile, coming forward with the box of goodies.

A STICKY TOFFEE CATASTROPHE

"I just wanted to say... I know you're just doing your job." She peeked up at him to see his warm, blue eyes gazing down at her.

He offered a smile, telling her, "I am. And I want you to know, I'm doing my best. I'm as anxious to clear Hannah as you are. I just have to do it properly, investigate every piece of evidence without prejudice."

Lucy nodded. That was nice to hear. "I did have a few ideas... "

Taylor's phone rang, and he held up a finger. "Just a minute. Hold that thought."

He picked up the receiver. "Taylor Baker." He listened for a moment, and then his lips curved slightly. He spoke softly, half turning away. "Hey, there. Can I call you back in a few minutes? Thanks." He hung up and turned back to Lucy, his expression suddenly guarded.

Lucy stiffened. She knew suddenly, with a woman's intuition, that it had been Charlene on the line.

"Taylor." Lucy struggled with the right way to bring the subject up. "I think you need to be careful with Charlene. I don't think she's being honest about her intentions."

Taylor's expression turned from friendly to cold in an instant. "Excuse me?" He raised his eyebrows.

Lucy bit her lip but continued. "What do you really know about her?"

Taylor stood up and crossed his arms. "So. You must have heard that we went to dinner together."

Lucy nodded. "But that's not why–"

Taylor interrupted her. "Lucy, I'm really glad you dropped by. I honestly don't want this investigation to come between us. But... you told me you weren't interested in dating me. I refuse to discuss the other women I date with you."

He walked to the door and opened it. "I've got to get back to work."

His message was clear. Lucy regretted bringing up Charlene before she'd had a chance to talk about the case with Taylor, but he'd never be receptive to her suggestions right now.

"OK," she said mildly, putting a pleasant expression on her face. "I'll see you later."

She walked out of the station, fighting the impulse to look back at him. Once she was back in her car, she blew out a breath, annoyed with the whole situation.

Charlene Tipton was hiding something, and Lucy was determined to find out what it was.

19

Lucy petted Gigi absently as she studied her laptop screen. The best way to clear Hannah's name was to find the real murderer, and so far, the only lead she had to work with was the bloody princess costume. She tapped in a search string with the costume's brand name, blanching when the results popped up.

Story Time costumes were carried in eight stores in this state alone! She drummed her fingers on the desk, causing Gigi to pounce. She scooped the Persian up off the desk, and set her down on her lap, keeping one hand busy stroking her fur. Gigi purred her approval.

It would be better if she could narrow the list down by suspect. She furrowed her brow, trying to remember where Bradley Carson and his wife lived. It was only a few towns over... She stared at a map of the area helplessly for a few minutes, then finally gave up and texted the question to Hannah.

A reply came almost immediately.

Lookout Falls

Lucy scrolled down the list of locations.

Her eyes widened as she saw the listing. There was a Story Time vendor in Lookout Falls!

Would her theory prove correct, that the murderer rented two princess costumes in different towns to throw off police?

Pulse racing, she started to punch the store's number into her phone, then glanced at the listing, her excitement fizzling out. Unlike Gina's shop, this shop was only open on weekends. She'd have to wait to contact them.

She huffed out a breath, considering her next move.

Hesitantly, she typed Charlene Tipton's name into the search bar, telling herself it wasn't jealousy she was feeling. She simply wanted to see if anything unusual popped up. The results were too numerous, so she added, "St. Paul".

Nothing. No results at all.

OK... Lucy thought for a minute, then cleared "St. Paul" and typed in "St. Petersburg".

Two results, but neither one fit the age bracket.

Lucy frowned, then typed, "Charlene Tipton Pet Grooming" with no specific location.

No results.

She clicked image search and scanned page after page of Charlene Tipton photos. None matched, and Lucy gave up after three pages, feeling like she was wasting her time.

Well, that didn't mean much, Lucy told herself, standing up and stretching. Not everyone was on social media or managed to get their name in the news. Stifling a yawn, she rummaged through a drawer for her nightgown, deciding to take a hot bath and get a good night's sleep.

Tomorrow was another day. Maybe they'd get some positive news on the investigation.

"READY TO FLEX YOUR SALES MUSCLES?" Lucy grinned at Betsy as they drove into town together, the back of the Lucy's SUV filled with small sample bags of Sweet Delight's Toffee.

Feeling powerless in the murder investigation, Lucy had decided to focus on her business today. She needed to drum up some revenue for Sweet Delights Bakery and had come up with a plan: dropping in on Ivy Creek's Main Street shops, to see if any shop owners would be willing to carry their new product.

Betsy had volunteered to join Lucy, to cover more ground in less time. Since sales were so slow, Aunt Tricia would be fine handling the front alone, while Hannah baked off a few items that were low in stock.

"Can I offer a quid pro quo deal?" inquired Betsy.

Lucy nodded, "Sure, just use your own judgement. Small displays would be better. We don't have a lot of space."

She thought that was a smart idea, though, and looked at Betsy approvingly. More shops might be more inclined to carry Sweet Delights' product if it were a mutually beneficial agreement. For some, that may even be worth more than the ten percent commission Lucy planned to offer.

They parked in a shady spot and Lucy opened the hatch. She and Betsy each took a tote bag full of samples and a handful of business cards.

"Meet you back here in an hour," Lucy called, heading east.

Betsy saluted and headed west.

Lucy stopped in at the bookstore first, chatting with the owner for a few minutes, and was rewarded with her first acceptance, agreeing to a ten percent commission. Encouraged by her success, she moved on to the music shop, the video store, and a consignment shop that carried chic, retro clothing. She received a little interest from the video store manager, who said she'd run it by the owner, but the other two declined.

Lucy stopped on the sidewalk beneath an elm tree and looked at her watch. Only time for one more shop. She scanned the street in front of her, skipping over the first two businesses. Gina's costume shop caught her eye.

It wouldn't hurt to try, she thought. If Gina was feeling chatty, she may be able to provide Lucy with more information about who rented the princess costumes. After all, Lucy's working theory of the killer renting an additional princess costume out of town extended to all the 'princesses' at the fair. It would be interesting to see the customer names, if Gina would be willing to share them.

She walked past the other shops and came to Party Time's door. Her enthusiasm fizzled as she noted the sign taped to the window. *Back in an hour!*

Lucy thought for a minute, then dug a pen and notepad out of her bag. She jotted a quick note, inviting Gina to carry Sweet Delights' toffee in her store for a ten percent commission. She wrapped the note around a business card and tucked it in the door. That was the best she could do for now.

Glancing at her watch, she hurried back to the car, finding Betsy waiting on a nearby bench.

The young woman jumped up as Lucy approached, with an excited expression on her face.

"Guess what?" she asked, her hazel eyes wide.

Lucy grinned. "Every shop you visited agreed to carry the toffee?"

Betsy shook her head. "Only two. No, this is about… the murder." Her voice lowered on the last words, and she glanced around.

Lucy unlocked the SUV, and the women slipped inside. Seated, Betsy turned to face her.

"I went into Franklin Flowers as my last stop. Guess who was in there, buying red roses?"

Lucy frowned, bewildered. She shook her head.

Betsy leaned forward. "Vince Byers! Doesn't that seem a little strange to you? He doesn't know anyone here in town. The flowers must have been for Tina Landon!"

Lucy was silent for a minute. Red roses… Not the kind of flowers you'd buy for a friend.

It was looking more and more like Tina was having an affair with her husband's business partner.

If it proved true, this could be the real motive behind Rex Landon's murder.

20

"Are you going to tell Taylor?" Aunt Tricia asked. She nibbled on an orange-coconut muffin, which she had deemed an appetizer for her lunch.

Lucy shook her head. She and Aunt Tricia were alone on the veranda, where the older woman was taking a break. Lucy had just finished filling her in on what Betsy had observed.

"No… I stopped by the station yesterday, and despite my best intentions, Taylor and I didn't exactly hit it off," Lucy remarked, hoping Aunt Tricia didn't ask for details.

"I need to give him a few days to cool down. But I was thinking I might stop in over at the flower shop and snoop a little bit. I need to bring some packages of toffee into town for the three businesses who agreed to carry it. All we handed out this morning were samples."

Aunt Tricia nodded; her eyes thoughtful as she looked out over the pretty scenery. Lucy followed her gaze, trying to envision the view as it would be in a few months' time. It was a depressing thought, but there were bigger issues at hand.

"How does Hannah seem to you?" Lucy asked, still concerned for her friend. Although Taylor had emphasized that he was trying to clear her name, Lucy knew it must be hard on Hannah, with a big chunk of the town acting as though she were a pariah.

"She's doing OK," Aunt Tricia assured her. "I'm glad she and her parents are close."

Lucy nodded, her thoughts flitting briefly to her own parents, now deceased. *What would they have made of this huge scandal that had the bakery stuck right smack in the middle?* She sighed. She was sure they would have stood by Hannah, the same as she, herself. Her parents had been good, loyal, people.

Footsteps could be heard approaching the veranda, and Lucy turned to see Betsy approaching. She held out a cordless phone.

"It's Gina," she announced with a huge smile, and Lucy knew it had to be good news.

She stood, walking toward the office with the receiver pressed to her ear.

"Hey, Gina. How are you?"

The woman's cheery voice came over the line. "Great! Sorry I missed you earlier. I love your new product, I tried some at the fair. Toffee has always been a weakness of mine. I'm definitely interested in carrying it."

Lucy smiled. "Awesome! Hey, I was going to swing through town in a few hours, on my way home. Will you be around, maybe at four o'clock? I can drop some by then."

"I sure will. See you in a bit," Gina replied, and hung up.

Lucy descended the stairs into the bakery's front room, encouraged by yet another acceptance. If the toffee started to sell at these other shops, that would go a long way towards adding some revenue.

"I HAVE JUST the place for these!" Gina said, accepting the bags of toffee and carrying them over to a small table. Lucy saw the shop owner had already set up a sign, advertising Sweet Delights Bakery's Toffee Candy.

The woman arranged the bundles, saying jokingly, "The hard part will be not eating them all myself."

Lucy smiled, her gaze wandering over the shop. Now that all the fair rentals had been returned, the racks were crowded. Costumes with fabrics in every imaginable color and texture hung side by side, velvet and gauzy lace competing with shimmering satin.

Gina followed her gaze. "Next big event is not until October," she announced. "It was nice to get a lot of summer sales for once."

Lucy turned to regard her with a hopeful expression. "I was wondering if you could do me a favor, Gina…"

The woman cocked her head, waiting.

"I really need to find out who rented princess costumes for the fair. Would it be possible to share that information with me?"

Gina was silent for a moment, looking away, then glanced at Lucy's face. "I really shouldn't, you know… but I do feel awful about what happened, with everyone spreading gossip about Hannah. I have to say, I'm still mystified with this interest in princess costumes from both you and Taylor. I mean, wasn't Hannah dressed as Robin Hood?"

Lucy nodded, hoping the woman didn't question her directly. So far, the police department had kept a lid on what exactly had been found in Sweet Delights' dumpster. The rumor had circulated that the murder weapon had been found, but so far, the news of the bloody princess costume had been kept secret. Lucy didn't want to be the one to disclose it.

Lucy's brows came together, in defense of her friend. "She was Robin Hood. And I can't stress strongly enough that Hannah is innocent."

Gina nodded. "I've known Hannah forever. There's no way she's guilty of murder. I sure hope Taylor can find the real killer."

Lucy persisted, "I can't tell you why, Gina, but it may go a long way toward proving Hannah's innocence if I could see who rented those costumes – specifically, the blue and yellow princess costumes."

Gina nodded and walked to the front counter, punching a few keys into her computer. "I have a list made up already. Taylor asked for the same thing. I guess it won't hurt to print you a copy."

Lucy was filled with gratitude, trying to appear patient as the printer spit out a sheet of paper. She took the document from Gina, folding it and tucking it into her purse.

"Thank you, so much." Lucy's voice was filled with sincerity. "I truly appreciate this."

Gina called out, "Good luck!" as Lucy took her leave, giving a little wave as she exited the shop.

As soon as she got into her vehicle, she took out the list, scanning it quickly. No names in particular jumped out at her. She'd look at it more carefully tonight, but right now she'd better hurry if she wanted to get to the flower shop before they closed.

Fifteen minutes later she was parking in front of Franklin Flowers. She took a deep breath as she entered the shop. *It smelled heavenly!* Her two favorite scents in the world were gardenias and chocolate chip cookies.

There was a woman Lucy didn't recognize at the counter. She turned with a smile, greeting Lucy.

"Good afternoon. We're closing in about twenty minutes, just so you're aware. Is there something I can help you with?"

Lucy had already planned what she would say. It may not have the desired result, but at least it would get the conversation rolling. "Yes, hello. I'm from Sweet Delights Bakery. My assistant, Betsy, was in here yesterday, and she said there was a man ahead of her buying red roses."

The woman nodded. "Yes, I remember your assistant. She was looking for shops to carry toffee candy."

Lucy smiled, mentally crossing her fingers. "Yes, right. When Betsy left, she approached that fellow and asked if he'd be interested in a gift bag of our toffee. To go with the flowers. You know, we give out complimentary samples sometimes." She was beginning to babble. She'd never been good at fibbing.

The shop owner wore a puzzled expression now, and Lucy hastened to finish. "To, ah, be delivered later today. Betsy can't remember the lady's name and we need it… for the tag. I thought you might be able to help."

The woman's expression suddenly brightened, and Lucy felt relieved.

"Oh, yes, I know exactly who you mean. And I do remember the lady's name. Well, her first name, at least," she said. "The gentleman asked me to provide a note card. Such a sweet message."

Lucy waited, her smile frozen in place, as the florist recited the message.

"Happy Birthday, Tina, from your big brother. I'll always be here for you."

21

Brother?

Lucy's expression must have shown her confusion, because the shop owner peered at Lucy's face curiously.

"Are you OK, miss?"

Lucy nodded woodenly. "I'm sorry," she said. "I just thought of something I need to do." She backed out of the shop, still processing the information. "Thank you," she said, distractedly, and turned to walk through the door.

A few steps down the sidewalk and Lucy was back in her vehicle. Automatically, she slid the keys into the ignition, but then just sat there, her thoughts buzzing.

Vince was Tina's brother?

She closed her eyes, trying to envision all the interactions she'd seen between the two. She'd been so sure they were a romantic pair! Now she realized she'd never seen Vince kiss Tina. He'd acted protective and supportive… and brotherly.

She sighed. Although she should probably run that information through a web search just to be certain, her gut instinct told her that this was the truth. Did that mean Vince and Tina didn't really have a motive to kill Rex Landon?

Well… not as a crime of passion, she supposed. But spouses were, after all, the first suspects. Still, this new information had moved the pair down on her suspect list, below Bradley and Valerie Carson.

She drove home slowly, her thoughts drifting to Taylor. She really wanted to see what he'd discovered in his investigation, but she knew he wouldn't be receptive to her questions. Or her theories, she realized sadly.

Even though Taylor was hopefully still working toward the same end - to clear Hannah's name - Lucy felt like she had to continue with her own investigation.

She could only rely on herself.

Lucy sipped at a cup of tea and unfolded Gina's list. She went through the names one by one, recognizing most of the last names as local families she'd known while growing up. Something seemed off, though, and she didn't realize what it was until the second time she'd gone through the list.

Charlene's name wasn't listed.

"That's odd," she muttered. Charlene, herself, had told Lucy that she'd rented her costume from Party Time, when she'd first arrived in town. Why wasn't she on the list? Was it just an oversight?

"What's odd?" asked Aunt Tricia, entering the kitchen. She opened the freezer and took out a container of ice cream.

"Gina provided me with a list of people who rented blue and yellow princess costumes, but Charlene's name isn't on it."

Aunt Tricia frowned. "That *is* odd." She took a bowl down from the cabinet and dug in the drawer for an ice cream scoop. Turning to Lucy, she suggested, "Why don't you call her?"

Lucy looked at the clock. It wasn't yet eight p.m. "Do you think that would be rude?" she asked. She didn't want to intrude on Gina's personal time.

Aunt Tricia shook her head. "She won't mind. Or I can call her if you want." Aunt Tricia and Gina were good friends, despite two decades of age difference, occasionally getting together on Wednesday nights to play cards.

Lucy hesitated. Aunt Tricia clucked her tongue and picked up the phone from the table, punching in the number from memory.

She held the phone to her ear, looking over at Lucy. "I know you, dear. You'll lie awake all night wondering about this."

The call connected, and Aunt Tricia spoke into the receiver. "Hi Gina, it's Tricia. Is it a bad time? OK, good. Listen, Lucy's going over that list you gave her. Didn't Charlene rent one of those costumes? Her name's not on the list."

She listened for a minute. "Uh-huh. Right. Do you recall it? Great! OK, no, I've got it. That's easy enough to remember. Thanks, Gina. You, too."

She hung up and turned to Lucy, setting down the phone. "It turns out Charlene Tipton is not her legal name. She had to use a credit card to rent the costume, and the credit card said Cheryl Ann Babcock. She told Gina she was in the process of getting her name changed legally. Something about a fresh start."

Lucy's brows shot up. *Charlene Tipton hadn't come up in her internet search because that wasn't her real name.*

She pushed her chair back from the table and hurried to her bedroom, powering up her computer. Aunt Tricia trailed behind her, spooning ice cream into her mouth.

"What are you doing?"

Lucy typed *Cheryl Ann Babcock* into the search bar and hit enter. "I'm looking up Charlene. There's something off about that woman."

"Let me know what you find." Aunt Tricia drifted off with her ice cream, in the direction of the living room.

Lucy scanned the hits that popped up. Even with a middle name included, there were more than a few, nationwide. Her eyes roamed over the cities first, looking for anything that started with "St."

Nothing.

Lucy added "Pet Grooming", and suddenly, there she was. Cheryl Ann Babcock, Professional Pet Groomer. She had a profile on a networking site for professionals.

Lucy tapped the link, looking at the "About" info for a hometown.

There it was.

It wasn't St. Paul or St. Petersburg, as she'd been expecting. It was a city not far from Ivy Creek, just over the state line.

Lucy recognized the name, although she had never been there.

Minton Heights. Little more than an hour away.

She stared at the screen, confused. *Was it the same woman?* She clicked on a picture, squinting at the screen. Yes. A little younger, maybe, but that was definitely Charlene Tipton.

She sat back, drumming her fingers on the table. *Why would the woman lie, and say she was from across the country?*

A fresh start. That's what Charlene had told Gina. Maybe she'd been involved in a bitter divorce or something. Lucy hesitated for a minute, feeling like she may be snooping for personal reasons, since Charlene was dating Taylor. After a moment of indecision, her curiosity won out. She typed 'Cheryl Ann Babcock, Minton Heights', and pressed enter.

An obituary came up, listing Cheryl as one of the surviving daughters of a Sadie Babcock, who had died almost ten months ago. Lucy scanned the obituary, seeing nothing else pertinent to Charlene. No mention of Charlene having kids of her own, or a husband. Only one sibling was listed, a sister named Jane. Sadie's cause of death wasn't listed.

Lucy cupped her chin in her hand, contemplating her next move. She was still not sure if any of this was relevant, but her curiosity was piqued. A sudden thought occurred to her, and she typed "Story Time costumes, Minton Heights" into the search.

Bingo! There was a Story Time vendor in that city; a shop called Once Upon a Party.

That clinched it. Lucy decided she'd drive out to Minton Heights tomorrow and see what she could find out.

After all, she reasoned, not only was Charlene a possible suspect in the murder, but she may also be guilty of something else... playing Taylor for a fool.

22

Lucy drove slowly through Minton Heights, on the lookout for Once Upon a Party. She'd gotten turned around once already in the strange town, full of one-way streets and impatient drivers honking their horns. A headache was beginning to spring up, and she was starting to wonder if this had been a bad idea.

There it was! Once Upon a Party.

Lucy managed to pull into the small parking lot just in time, twisting the wheel sharply and earning an irritated beep from the car directly behind her.

"Sorry," she called out automatically, though her window was up. She zoomed into a space right in front of the shop, surprised to see only one other car. It was a Saturday afternoon, but apparently there wasn't much of a need for party supplies today in Minton Heights.

She flipped down the visor and checked her reflection, wondering how she should approach the subject of Cheryl

Anne Babcock. Lucy sighed. She was really terrible at fibbing.

She racked her brain for a plausible story as she exited the car and approached the shop. Nothing came to her. She decided to just wing it.

A bell rang as the door opened, and Lucy stepped inside, taking a moment for her eyes to get accustomed to the dim interior, a stark contrast to the bright sunlight.

"May I help you?"

A woman's voice came from the back of the store and Lucy swiveled her head, trying to locate the source. She finally spied a diminutive blond woman between the racks of costumes. She must have stood only an inch or two over five feet tall. Lucy smiled in response and walked in her direction.

"Hello," Lucy's gaze wandered over the costumes, and she hit upon an idea. "I'm looking for a shop that could rent out quite a few of one particular costume. It's for a bridal shower. We're all going to dress as princesses, kind of as an inside joke."

The woman gave her a curious look, but smiled, nonetheless. "OK, I don't hear that every day. But I do have princess costumes. How many do you need?"

Lucy stalled, thinking. "Well... we've decided on the Story Time blue and yellow ones. Do you carry those?"

The woman nodded, though her smile seemed to fade a bit. "Yes, I do." She repeated her question. "How many do you need?"

Lucy hesitated. *This was the tricky part.* "Um... how many did you say you have?"

The woman regarded Lucy silently for a moment. "Five," she finally answered. Her face seemed shuttered as she waited for Lucy's response.

Lucy replied, thinking fast. "I actually need six. Do you have any that are about to be returned? We haven't quite set a date for the bridal shower yet, so we could wait."

The woman frowned and shook her head. "Five. That's all I have."

Lucy was afraid the woman was beginning to regard her suspiciously. Aiming to appear casual, Lucy laughed and said, "Well, maybe we'll have to choose a different costume. Do you have six of anything in stock?"

The shopkeeper turned to eye her costume racks. "I have six Wonder Woman costumes... six belly dancers.... six female pirates—"

Lucy interrupted her. "Maybe I'll check with my friends first and give you a call back."

The woman nodded, and turned back to her task, organizing the costumes on the rack in front of her.

Lucy turned to go, walking slowly, wondering if she should push her luck.

Why not?

She stopped and turned, addressing the shopkeeper again. "I do have a question you might be able to help me with. Do you know a Cheryl Ann Babcock?"

The woman's hands stilled. She turned, pinning Lucy with a malevolent stare.

"Who did you say you were?" Her voice was hard and unfriendly, and Lucy swallowed nervously.

"I… I didn't. Um… I just remember Cheryl from way back in the day. I was wondering if she still lived here?"

The shopkeeper shook her head. "Never heard of her," she said dismissively, deliberately turning her back on Lucy. The message was clear. Lucy had taken up enough of her time and was no longer welcome.

Lucy turned around again and left the store, wondering what that was all about. She'd bet her last dime that the woman was hiding something. *But what?*

Stumped, she drove out of the parking lot, unsure of where she was going. Her head was beginning to throb, and Lucy decided an afternoon jolt of caffeine might do the trick. She spotted a diner and pulled in. She'd regroup over a cup of coffee.

The diner was pleasantly bright and clean, with art déco black-and-white tiles on the floor and leather swivel stools lined up in a neat row. Lucy sighed as she settled into a seat at the counter, picking up the menu to look it over.

A middle-aged waitress, with red hair threaded with silver, appeared in front of her. She wore bright red lipstick and a genuinely friendly expression.

"Hey, there. What can I get you?" She stood poised, order pad and pen at the ready.

Lucy scanned the items. She might feel better with a sandwich in her system. "I'll have a grilled cheese and tomato on wheat, please. And a cup of coffee with cream and sugar."

The waitress grinned and snapped her pad shut, tucking it away in her apron pocket. "Coming up in a jiffy," she said.

She returned in a moment with Lucy's coffee, setting it down on the counter. It smelled delicious, and Lucy sipped the beverage, feeling better already.

"Oh, yes…" She sighed gratefully. "Thank you. I really needed that." Lucy smiled at her, getting a good vibe from the friendly face. The woman's name tag read Kelly.

"Had a rough day?" Kelly asked, wiping down the counter.

Lucy saw the short order cook behind her assembling Lucy's sandwich, and her stomach growled. He slapped it down on the grill and she could hear it sizzle from where she sat.

Lucy inclined her head. "Seems like a long day, is all. Are you from Minton Heights?"

Kelly nodded, refilling the straw dispenser. "Yep. Born here, raised here. Probably die here. But not for a while yet," she said with a wink at Lucy.

Lucy took another sip of her coffee. After the cold reception to her question at the costume shop, she was almost afraid to ask any questions. She eyed the cook plating up her sandwich, deciding she'd eat first.

It was surprisingly good, and Lucy finished every last bite, washing the sandwich down with the rest of her coffee. She gathered up the bill and headed to the register, seeing Kelly cross the room to meet her there. Lucy settled up, tipping

A STICKY TOFFEE CATASTROPHE

Kelly a few dollars, then decided she may as well ask her question. She had nothing to lose at this point.

"I'm hoping you can help me," she began. "I'm trying to find an old friend... Cheryl Ann Babcock. Do you know her, by any chance?" She hoped Kelly didn't ask her why.

Kelly nodded, her brown eyes turning sad. "I do. But I hate to tell you, Cheryl Ann hasn't been around much since the tragedy. She took it real hard. I'm not sure she even lives in town anymore."

Lucy absorbed the information. "Do you mean the passing of her mother?"

Kelly nodded her head, sighing. "We all couldn't believe it, that Sadie would... well... I mean, I'd never known anyone, personally, before, that committed suicide. Such a shock."

Lucy nodded sympathetically, her heart beating fast. She felt like she was getting close to some answers. *Was this the reason for Charlene's fresh start in Ivy Creek?*

"So tragic," Lucy agreed softly, looking down. She glanced back up at Kelly, speaking softly, "I didn't hear much about the cause of death. Does anyone know why Sadie killed herself?"

Kelly looked troubled. "There was no suicide note. But she'd been so distressed after that unscrupulous developer practically stole her house out from under her... Well, I know that's who the girls blame, anyway. According to her daughters, Sadie would still be alive if it weren't for Rex Landon."

Lucy's ears rang and she felt numb. *Rex Landon had swindled Charlene's mother out of her home.* She opened her mouth to speak, but no words came out.

Kelly looked inquiringly at Lucy. "Do you know Jane? Cheryl Ann's sister? She might know where to find her."

Still speechless, Lucy simply shook her head.

Kelly pointed out the window. "Jane has a shop about a block away. You can't miss it. It's called Once Upon a Party."

23

Lucy stumbled out of the diner, her thoughts racing. Blindly, she unlocked her car and slid into the seat, gripping the steering wheel, and staring into space.

The unfriendly shopkeeper was Charlene's sister.

Charlene had taken one of Jane's blue and yellow princess costumes, Lucy was sure of it. The same costume that later turned up in Sweet Delights Bakery's dumpster, splashed with Rex Landon's blood.

Charlene was the killer. And possibly Jane had been her accomplice.

Two people could have committed the murder more easily than one, Lucy remembered Hannah pointing out. One person to disable the generator, the other to stab Rex in the back.

Lucy reversed out of the parking lot and headed back to Ivy Creek, going over all the details. She would have to be sure everything fit before she told Taylor what she suspected. If not, he wouldn't even listen. He'd just accuse Lucy of being jealous over his dating Charlene.

The way Lucy saw it, Rex Landon had conned Sadie Babcock the same way he'd conned the Carsons, taking advantage of an elderly woman and coercing her to sign a dubious contract. Who knows? Maybe he'd even gone farther in his shady dealings. Whatever had happened, Sadie had become so distraught after losing her home that she'd committed suicide. Her girls blamed Rex Landon and conspired to get their revenge.

Lucy remembered Charlene at the fair, telling Rex he must be mistaken, that they'd never met before. *That must be why she'd been wearing a mask*, Lucy realized. She'd needed to get close enough to Rex without him recognizing her.

A sudden thought struck Lucy. *It had all been a sham.* Charlene Tipton was not in Ivy Creek to settle down and run a pet grooming shop. She had followed Rex Landon there with the intent to kill him.

She recalled Charlene on the phone, saying, "Another six weeks in this godforsaken town is all I can stand." *Had she been talking to Jane?* It sounded like Charlene had decided six weeks after the murder was long enough to avoid suspicion, before she ultimately left town.

Lucy's next thought troubled her heart. *Had Charlene started dating Taylor to stay close to the investigation?*

She reached for her phone, setting it in the hands-free holder as she took the on ramp for the freeway.

"Call Taylor–" she instructed the voice command app. A half-second later, she changed her mind, saying, "Cancel," before the call could go through.

Taylor wouldn't believe her. She needed to tell Aunt Tricia, Betsy, Joseph, and Hannah. They could all go into the police station together. That way, the conversation couldn't turn into a personal issue between herself and Taylor. They would, as a group, make their suspicions known, and the Ivy Creek Police Department would be forced to take them seriously and investigate Charlene Tipton.

"Call Aunt Tricia," Lucy instructed the app. She heard the phone ringing, but Aunt Tricia didn't pick up.

Lucy glanced at the clock. The bakery had closed, though she knew Hannah was planning to stay after hours tonight to make more toffee. Aunt Tricia must be on the road. She never answered her phone when she was driving.

Lucy decided to leave a message. "Hi, it's me. I just found some evidence that almost certainly implicates Charlene in the murder. I don't want to call Taylor—I want us to all go in together, and then he'll have to listen. I'll be home in less than an hour, and I'll tell you all about it then. I'm going to stop by the bakery first to tell Hannah."

Lucy hit the button to end the call, calling home next, on the off chance that Aunt Tricia had already arrived. There was no answer there, either. She disconnected, letting her mind circle around the case.

Had Jane been at the fair, also? Maybe she had been the one to carry the murder weapon on her person. *Was it Jane that had stolen one of Hannah's arrows?* It would have been riskier for Charlene to do so, as she might have been spotted by someone from Sweet Delights Bakery. Jane could have wandered through the fair quite anonymously. And with the access she had to her choice of costumes, she could have found one that would conceal both a knife and an arrow.

Then she would have met up with Charlene behind the bandstand, and waited for the right moment...

Lucy's phone rang, interrupting her thoughts. "Answer," she instructed the voice app, assuming the call was from Aunt Tricia.

White noise filled the car's interior with vague, unidentifiable sounds in the background. A few clanging sounds sounding far away, but it was mostly static. Lucy glanced quickly at the caller ID.

The call wasn't from Aunt Tricia; it was from the bakery.

That was odd. It must be Hannah.

"Hello?" Lucy exclaimed. "Hannah, are you there?"

No reply. "Hello? Hello?" Lucy repeated, but all she heard was white noise.

"Disconnect," Lucy instructed. As soon as the call ended, Lucy said, "Call bakery."

The line was busy. Lucy ended the call, then tried several times more.

The line stayed busy.

It was after hours. There was no reason for the line to be busy.

Lucy frowned. She accelerated slightly, traveling just a hair over the speed limit now.

She'd be at the bakery in fifteen minutes, she told herself, trying to ignore the uneasy feeling that raised goosebumps on her arms.

It was probably nothing.

24

Lucy wheeled into Sweet Delight's parking lot, peering anxiously at the storefront windows. The front room's lights were out, and the "Closed" sign was hanging on the door. She was relieved to see everything looked as it should. Behind the counter, light was spilling from the entryway that led to the kitchen in back. Hannah must still be here working, parked in the rear lot, as was her habit. *Wait till she hears what I found out*, Lucy thought. *She won't believe it!*

Lucy unlocked the door and let herself in, calling out.

"Hannah! Guess what?"

She couldn't wait to clear her friend's name. As soon as she could gather Betsy, Joseph, and Hannah at her house with Aunt Tricia, and fill everyone in, they would go to the police station tonight. There was no time to waste. Charlene's sister Jane had seemed very suspicious of her questions. Lucy guessed it was only a matter of time before both women decided to flee.

"Hannah?" Lucy called again.

She reached over and flipped on the lights, walking toward the kitchen. As she passed behind the counter, she saw the telephone receiver, out of its cradle, lying on top of the glass bakery case. She picked the handset up and held it to her ear, hearing a dial tone. Someone must have forgotten to hang it up, she realized, setting the phone in the charger. *Maybe Aunt Tricia had dialed Lucy's number and then gotten distracted.* Her aunt was starting to become a little forgetful.

She passed through the doorway leading to the work area, wondering where Hannah was. The restroom, maybe?

Lucy's eyes wandered over the empty kitchen, taking in several shallow pans of toffee cooling on the workbench. She frowned, suddenly spotting a mess on the floor.

The copper-bottomed saucepan lay tipped over on the tile, with a pool of sticky toffee spread out beneath it. A wire whisk and wooden spoon lay on the floor nearby. A few feet away lay the rolling pin.

What a mess. Hannah must have bumped the pot off the stove accidentally. No doubt she was upstairs in the storeroom getting supplies to clean it up.

Well... accidents happen. I hope none of it spattered on her skin, Lucy thought, concerned. *Liquid toffee can give you a bad burn.*

At least she had good news to share with Hannah, and she was sure Hannah would welcome a helping hand in cleaning up the sticky mess.

Lucy turned around, intending to head for the stairs, when she heard a muffled thud. Puzzled, she turned back to survey the kitchen. She swiveled her head, hearing the sound again. *Where could it be coming from?*

A STICKY TOFFEE CATASTROPHE

Thud... thud.

Her gaze landed on the walk-in freezer at the far end of the room. Slowly, Lucy walked toward it, wondering if perhaps the fan blades were clogged with ice. Maybe that would account for the strange noise.

As she got closer, she was alarmed to hear a muffled voice coming from inside, accompanied by another dull thud. Shocked, she rushed to the door and yanked it open.

She was horrified to see Hannah, slumped on the metal floor, her hands bound to the built-in freezer rack with twine.

"Oh my God!" Lucy rushed inside, kneeling on the cold floor beside her friend. Hannah was bleeding from a cut on her head, and her eyes were slow to focus.

"Lucy?" she asked, wincing as she raised her head. She was shivering all over, Lucy noted with alarm, wondering how long Hannah had been in there.

"I'm right here, Hannah," Lucy answered, instructing her, "Hold still."

Lucy's hands trembled as she struggled with the knots in the twine. She needed to call the police and an ambulance, but she couldn't leave Hannah in here for one more second.

Lucy got one knot free and fumbled with the second one, her fingers going numb.

What had happened? Was it a burglary? Or had Charlene done this? Why attack Hannah?

"Hannah, who did this?"

As much as she wanted her friend to conserve her energy, Lucy had to know if they were still in danger.

"Hannah?"

Panicked, Lucy looked down at Hannah's ashen face, realizing the young woman had lost consciousness.

"No, no, no!" Lucy abandoned the remaining knot and put her ear to Hannah's mouth, relieved to find her still breathing. But Hannah's breathing was shallow and uneven, and Lucy was afraid she didn't have much time.

She bit her lip, making a hard decision. She'd have to leave Hannah for a minute and run to get her kitchen shears. This knot was hopeless.

She'd grab the telephone while she was in the kitchen and hit 911, but she'd leave the handset on the counter. She knew that a phone wouldn't work inside a steel refrigeration unit. After she'd placed the call, she wouldn't need to stay on the line. The authorities would come.

"Hannah," Lucy spoke softly, bending over her friend's pallid face. She didn't know if Hannah could hear her. "I promise, I'll be right back."

Straightening up, Lucy spun around, and in two steps had reached the door, giving it a push.

It didn't budge.

Lucy placed both hands flat on the frigid steel panel and shoved with all her might, bringing her right foot up to bear on it as well. The door made a light rattling sound but didn't give. Lucy's heart leapt into her throat, and she tried not to panic.

She had to get them out of here!

She looked out through the door's small glass window, despairing.

A face suddenly popped up outside, just inches from the glass, and Lucy recoiled in horror, stumbling backward.

It was Charlene, with a malevolent grin twisting her pretty features. Her grin slowly morphed into a pouty face, and she pressed her lips to the frosty glass in a grotesque parody of a kiss.

She stepped back and gave Lucy a little wave, then held an object up for Lucy to see.

It was the key to the freezer's padlock.

Charlene had locked them in.

25

*L*ucy pounded on the door.

"Charlene! You can't leave us in here! Hannah's hurt!"

She pressed her face close to the glass, unsure if Charlene could hear her.

"Let us out, Charlene. Just tie us up and go. You'll get a head start! No one knows anything yet, I swear." Her voice was pleading, but Charlene turned away, unaffected.

Through her vantage point of the freezer's window, Lucy could see the woman walking back through the kitchen, stepping delicately around the mess on the floor.

Defeated, Lucy turned her attention back to Hannah. *She had to do something to warm Hannah up.* Lucy looked around the freezer, her eyes traveling over the walls. Up high in the corner, there was a metal box with a group of insulated wires stemming from it. The wiring ran the length of the ceiling

A STICKY TOFFEE CATASTROPHE

and wall joint, ending behind the fan. She knew nothing about the mechanics of walk-in freezers, but maybe if she yanked out all the wires…

She stepped over and stood on tiptoe, barely able to reach the box. With a short prayer that she didn't electrocute herself, she grasped the bundle of wires and pulled hard.

Immediately, the lights and the fan cut off. Lucy immediately felt more hopeful, without the fan blasting frigid air onto her face. It was dark, though, with the only light coming in through the small window on the door.

After a minute, her eyes adjusted and she stepped over to Hannah, stooping down to check her pulse. Sighing with relief when she felt it beating under her fingertips, she then spoke loudly, hoping to rouse her.

"Hannah! Wake up, Hannah."

In a flash of inspiration, Lucy removed her own blouse. It was lightweight, and only three-quarter sleeved, but it was warm from her body. She'd worn a lacy camisole under it, and she silently blessed her wardrobe choice that morning. She wound the garment over Hannah's head and neck, fashioning a sort of hood. If she could keep Hannah's head warm, that might help. Task accomplished, Lucy blew on her fingers to warm them and began to work on the binding's second knot again.

After a few minutes, her hard work was rewarded, and she felt the knot begin to loosen.

"C'mon…" she whispered, once more cupping her icy fingers near her mouth to thaw them with her breath, before continuing her attempt.

Yes! The knot suddenly came free, and Lucy quickly unwound the twine binding Hannah's wrists. Reaching under her friend's armpits, Lucy gently moved her to the center of the floor, sitting and pulling Hannah into her embrace. She wrapped her arms around the other woman from behind, alarmed at how chilled Hannah's skin felt. Banishing all negative thoughts and fears from her mind, she concentrated on warming her, briskly rubbing Hannah's arms.

It worked. Hannah began to stir.

"Lucy?" she mumbled. "Why is it so dark in here?"

"I pulled the wires to stop the fan," Lucy answered, relieved to hear Hannah's voice. "Charlene locked us in."

Hannah groaned, and Lucy stiffened with alarm. "Are you OK?"

Hannah was silent for a few seconds, then chuckled softly. "Not really, no," she answered, with her usual dry wit. "I'd kill for a cup of hot chocolate."

Lucy's lips curved into a smile, despite the circumstances. Hannah seemed to be regaining her senses.

Hannah twisted in her arms, looking up at her. "I'm so sorry, Lucy. This is all my fault."

"Hush…" Lucy said. "It is not."

Hannah continued. "I feel so stupid. Charlene came into the bakery right before closing, saying she wanted to look through our cake album. Tricia had planned to stop by the bookstore on her way home, so I told her to go ahead. I was going to be here a while making toffee, anyway."

A STICKY TOFFEE CATASTROPHE

Lucy prompted, "What happened then? I saw the toffee and saucepan on the floor."

Hannah sighed. "Charlene asked if she could use the bakery phone, since she'd forgotten hers. I said, sure, and let her come behind the counter. But then I turned my back on her to work on the stove. Next thing I knew, I woke up in here, tied to the rack with my head hurting. I think she must have sneaked up behind me and hit me with something."

An uncontrollable shiver went through Hannah, and Lucy hugged her closer.

"I think she smacked you with the rolling pin," she informed her friend. "I saw it on the floor."

Hannah grunted. After a minute, she commented, "So I'm guessing Charlene killed Rex Landon, and she thought I was a threat."

Now it was Lucy's turn to feel guilty. "I think I may have had something to do with that. This is what I found out today…"

After she'd related the day's events, including the fact that Jane had become suspicious of her, Hannah murmured softly, "I bet Jane called Charlene on her cell the minute you left. Coming to the bakery at closing and using our telephone was just a ruse to catch me with my guard down."

"But why come after you?" Lucy countered. "Unless…" She suddenly realized Charlene had been the one to call her from the bakery line to lure her there.

"Charlene knew I'd come looking for you. The good thing is, I called Aunt Tricia before I came here. She knows I found evidence that implicates Charlene. And Aunt Tricia knew I was coming here. Eventually she'll call the police." *Or come looking for me herself*, Lucy realized, with sudden dread.

Her teeth began to chatter, and she knew she had to get up and move.

"I want to look out the window," Lucy said. "Will you be OK if I move?"

Hannah nodded, and Lucy carefully scooted out from behind her. She stepped over to the window and looked out.

"See anything?"

Lucy began to shake her head no, when suddenly Charlene came into view. Lucy shrank back slightly, but the woman wasn't looking at her.

Charlene was facing the bakery's rear door, backing away, her posture and face filled with panic. It was like watching a movie with the sound off.

Lucy whispered, "I think something's happening."

A glimmer of hope rose in her. *Could it be?*

She pressed her face to the window, rubbing her chilled arms, witnessing Charlene turn to flee. The woman crashed into the flour bin and knocked it over, pluming the air with a white cloud before scrambling away, out of Lucy's view.

"What is it?" Hannah asked, her voice shaking with the cold.

Lucy's spirits soared as she saw the trademark blue uniform of Ivy Creek's police force appear in her line of sight. Three officers swarmed the bakery, guns in hand.

"The police are here!" Lucy exclaimed, pounding on the door with both fists. "Help! Help!" She kicked the door for good measure.

Hannah joined in, yelling and kicking the side wall of the unit from where she lay.

"Help us!" the women shouted together.

Suddenly, a familiar face filled the window.

Taylor.

He looked shocked to see Lucy and Hannah, and she felt the steel door rattle as he pulled at it.

"Charlene has the key!" Lucy yelled, hoping the woman hadn't escaped.

Taylor nodded, his blue eyes meeting hers. He held up a finger and disappeared.

Lucy tried to calm her racing heart. *Key or no key, Taylor would get them out.*

She crouched beside Hannah, taking her chilled hands to warm them.

"Ready to break out of here?" She peered worriedly at the oozing cut on Hannah's head, trying to convince herself everything would be OK now.

Hannah grinned weakly, though her teeth chattered. "Yeah. You owe me a hot chocolate."

At that moment, the freezer door opened behind her, and Lucy turned to see Taylor rushing in.

He scooped Lucy up in his arms, calling for an ambulance. His gruff, authoritative voice was the most welcome thing Lucy had ever heard.

"Thank God, you're OK," he murmured, carrying her out into the brightly lit bakery.

Over his shoulder, she could see Charlene being led away by two officers, handcuffed, with her head hanging low. Lucy watched, blinking away tears, as another officer carried Hannah out of the freezer, his uniform coat draped over her shoulders.

Lucy closed her eyes, taking comfort in the warmth and safety of Taylor's embrace.

26

"It took eleven stitches to close the wound, but Hannah will be fine," the doctor informed them, and a collective sigh of relief went through the room. "No signs of hypothermia, but I'd like to keep her overnight, in case of a concussion."

Hannah's parents had met them at the hospital, along with Aunt Tricia, and they had all been on pins and needles in the waiting room. Taylor had insisted that Lucy be checked out as well, but, as she had jokingly told the paramedics, nothing had been injured but her pride. She couldn't believe she'd let her guard down, knowing that Charlene was dangerous.

"Can we see her?" asked Mrs. Curry, clutching at her husband's hand.

The doctor nodded, and the pair went into Hannah's room. Lucy, Aunt Tricia, and Taylor decided to give them a few moments alone with their daughter.

"What will happen to Charlene now?" asked Aunt Tricia. Lucy had filled them both in on all the details she'd found out while in Minton Heights.

Taylor's voice was grim. "We got a full confession, which implicated her sister as an accomplice. We alerted the authorities in Minton Heights, and they managed to catch Jane just as she was trying to leave town. Both women will be charged with the murder of Rex Landon, and Charlene will be charged with the attempted murder of Hannah and Lucy as well."

Lucy cocked her head. "Not just assault? Will an attempted murder charge stick?"

Taylor looked at her, his eyes sober. "Charlene had every intention of killing you both, Lucy. She confessed on tape that she planned to wait until you were both weak with hypothermia, then drag Hannah back out of the freezer, stage her suicide, and set fire to the bakery. She thought it would look like Hannah went crazy, locking you in the freezer, and then killing herself. In her own words, *'the whole town thinks Hannah is a murderer, anyway.'* "

Aunt Tricia huffed out her displeasure. "Well, that will change, and not a moment too soon! This town will be eating crow for not standing behind one of their own."

Hannah's parents came out of the room, their faces sagging with relief.

"She's asking for you, Lucy," Mrs. Curry said, tucking a tissue into her bag.

"*And* a cup of hot chocolate," Mr. Curry smiled, though his face was weary. "We're going to try and rustle one up in the cafeteria."

A STICKY TOFFEE CATASTROPHE

Lucy, Taylor, and Aunt Tricia entered the hospital room, and Lucy's heart squeezed, seeing Hannah, pale and fragile looking, propped up on pillows in the bed. She greeted them with a wan smile. The nurse had shaved an area of her scalp, and a thick gauze bandage was secured around her head.

"Hey, you," Lucy smiled down at her. "How are you feeling?"

"Better than I look," Hannah joked. "This isn't a great hairstyle for me."

Aunt Tricia stood on the other side of the bed, patting Hannah's arm. "We're just so glad you're going to be OK, dear."

Hannah caught Lucy's eye, with a rare serious expression. "You saved my life with your quick thinking, Lucy. Disabling the fan, and wrapping my head…"

Lucy shrugged, deflecting the praise with humor. "You're my best employee. I couldn't run the bakery without you." Her words were light, but her heart was filled with gratitude for their narrow escape.

Just then, Betsy came bustling through the door.

"Oh, Hannah, your head!" she cried out, rushing to the bedside. "Are you OK?"

"Nothing a little rest won't cure," Hannah assured her.

"And eleven stitches," reminded Taylor.

Lucy looked around. "Where's Joseph?" The two were practically inseparable these days.

Betsy replied, "Oh, he wanted to stop in the gift shop for something to cheer Hannah up." She addressed Hannah. "I told him no flowers; just in case you were allergic."

Hannah smiled. "That's sweet of him. Speaking of allergies, how goes it with the cats?"

Betsy beamed a brilliant smile. "I went to an allergist, and the results came in today. Guess what? I'm not allergic to cats after all! The doctor says it's something in Joseph's carpet. So, he's planning to pull up all the carpet and put down hardwood flooring." She looked so pleased that Lucy couldn't help but smile.

Mrs. Curry appeared in the doorway, holding a Styrofoam cup. "Guess what I've got... besides this?" She brought the cup to Hannah, peeling back the tab on the lid.

Hannah sipped, her eyes closing as she savored the beverage. "Whatever it is, it can't be as good as this."

Mrs. Curry's eyes sparkled. "Oh, yes, it can!" She looked around the room at all of them.

"I just got off the phone with Mrs. Carson. Bradley hired a lawyer who went over that sale contract with a fine-tooth comb. He found a loophole that will effectively void the contract... I didn't understand all that legalese... but, whatever it was, when his lawyer brought it to the attention of Mr. Landon's business partner, the company decided to pull out. They've decided to move on to a different town and find a new location for their office park."

"So, the Carsons won't have to leave their home!" exclaimed Hannah, a huge smile on her face.

"And Sweet Delights Bakery won't have an ugly office park across from it!" Aunt Tricia chimed in.

Lucy grinned, looking around the room at all the happy faces. *It looked like everything was going their way.*

She watched Taylor as he joked with Hannah, teasing her about her chocolate addiction. Flashing back to the moment she'd seen Taylor's face in that small, frosty window, she examined her feelings. Taylor was always there for her, rescuing her from more than a few hairy predicaments. The silly arguments they occasionally had were shallow compared to the depth of their friendship.

In short, Taylor Baker was more precious to her than he knew.

Maybe it was time for that to change, she thought. He looked her way just then, his blue eyes twinkling as he caught her watching him. He grinned, and Lucy smiled back, making a decision.

She was ready to take a chance on romance again.

She would open her heart back up to Taylor and see where it led.

The End

SWEET DELIGHTS BAKERY'S CHOCOLATE ALMOND TOFFEE CANDY

Ingredients

1 cup chopped toasted almonds, separated into 2/3 cup and 1/3 cup
1 cup butter (not margarine)
1 cup granulated sugar
1 cup mini chocolate chips
½ tsp. salt
1 tsp. pure vanilla extract

Procedure

Grease a 9" square baking pan and line the bottom with parchment. Flip the parchment back over so it's greased on the top. Sprinkle 2/3 cup of almonds evenly over the surface.

In a 3-quart heavy saucepan, melt the butter over low heat. Turn the heat up to medium and add the sugar and salt, stirring constantly with a whisk until the sugar dissolves.

Continue cooking, stirring occasionally (and gently) with a wooden spoon, until the mixture reaches 295 degrees F on a candy thermometer. Do not over-stir, or you will have bubbles in the finished candy.

Remove from heat and stir in the vanilla extract. Pour the hot mixture over the almonds in the pan and let it set for five minutes. Scatter the mini chocolate chips over the surface evenly and cover the pan with foil to trap the heat. Wait just a minute or two until the chocolate starts to melt. Spread the chocolate out with a spatula or back of a spoon, coating the entire surface. Sprinkle the remaining almonds on top.

Let toffee sit at room temperature for two hours. (If the chocolate still is tacky, refrigerate for fifteen minutes before cutting)

Invert the pan to release the candy. Flip it back over, chocolate side up, and break apart with a sharp knife.

Store at room temperature in a sealed container.

Yield: approx. 15 pieces

AFTERWORD

Thank you for reading A Sticky Toffee Catastrophe. I really hope you enjoyed reading it as much as I had writing it!

If you have a minute, please consider leaving a review on Amazon or the retailer where you got it.

Many thanks in advance for your support!

DOUGH SHALL NOT MURDER

CHAPTER 1 SNEAK PEEK

CHAPTER 1 SNEAK PEEK

"Fall is my favorite season," sighed Betsy, blissfully sipping her pumpkin latte. "Don't get me wrong—summer's great! But something about the leaves changing color, and the night air becoming crisp..."

Lucy grinned at her young employee, who had decided to taste-test the bakery's new seasonal coffee flavor. "And pumpkin everything! The pumpkin chocolate-chip muffins are our top seller. They're selling out as quickly as Hannah bakes them."

Hannah came through the kitchen door at that moment, bearing a tray of pastries. "These guys might be a contender, though." She set the tray down for Lucy's inspection. "Caramel apple tartlets."

"Those are almost too pretty to eat," Aunt Tricia commented. She chose one, holding it up to admire the fancy fluted crust. "But not quite." She bit into the pastry, murmuring her approval. Swallowing, she complimented Hannah. "Oh, my, these are divine!"

Hannah beamed and finished filling the glass pastry case. Turning to Lucy, she asked, "What's next, boss?" Her eyes twinkled. She and Lucy were old high school chums. When Lucy had taken over Sweet Delights Bakery upon the untimely passing of her parents, Hannah had stepped in to become the assistant baker.

Lucy glanced at the clock. "We still have fifteen minutes before opening. Let's go ahead and put up some Halloween decorations." She retrieved a box from under the front counter and brought it over to a table. The ladies crowded around as she opened it.

Betsy's eyes lit up. She reached in to pull out a string of mini lights shaped like pumpkins. "How adorable! These will look perfect in the front window!"

Aunt Tricia spied the electric Jack O' Lantern and lifted that out next. "I think this will be just the thing for upstairs on the veranda." She headed in that direction as Lucy unpacked a few more decorations. A small, poseable skeleton… two gauzy ghosts about ten inches tall, equipped with loops to hang them…

Hannah laughed and held up a rubber bat suspended on a clear line. She flipped a switch on its back and the bat's eyes glowed red. "This guy is pretty spooky!"

Lucy chuckled and peered at the remaining items in the box. An assortment of colorful, synthetic fall leaves, and a scarecrow which would need to be snapped together. "I think these leaves will look great scattered in the front window, with the ghosts above them. The scarecrow can stand outside at the entrance, and we'll hang the skeleton on the inside of the door."

DOUGH SHALL NOT MURDER

They each proceeded with their tasks, chatting conversationally.

"I met Joseph's younger brother, Derek, last night," Betsy announced, tacking up one end of the light string. "Such a nice guy! He's a freshman at Hawthorn College, a theater major." Betsy was dating Joseph Hiller, who was the Ivy Creek Theater's production manager.

"Theatre must be in the Hiller's blood," remarked Lucy. "Will Derek be in the November production of The Sword and the Stone?" She was looking forward to going to that play. The story of King Arthur had always been one of her favorite tales.

Betsy nodded, looping the string into a swag, and securing the midpoint. "He's trying for the lead. He'd make a great young King Arthur." She looked over at Lucy, grinning, "I think he'll stop by soon and you'll get to meet him. I mentioned pumpkin muffins to him, and he practically drooled."

"We'll have to save him one," Hannah called out to Betsy with a smile. She finished hanging up the bat and ghosts and got down from the chair she'd dragged over. "What do you guys think?"

Lucy nodded approvingly as Betsy finished stringing her lights and came to stand beside her. "Looks great, guys." She eyed the front window where she'd scattered the leaves. "Hannah, I think you and I should make an edible spooky house for the window display, too. The kids will love that."

Hannah grinned. "Sounds like fun!"

Aunt Tricia walked into the room, returning from upstairs. She looked at what they'd accomplished, and a smile curved her lips. "Well, ladies, I think we're ready for Halloween!" Glancing at the clock, she added, "And for business, too." She unlocked the door and flipped the sign to "Open", while Lucy positioned the scarecrow and skeleton.

Betsy returned to her station behind the front counter, organizing the flavored syrups next to the coffee machines, and Aunt Tricia opened the cash register, stocking it with bills. Hannah and Lucy stood in front of the pastry case, discussing their baking plans for the day.

"How many of those new caramel apple tartlets did you make?" Lucy asked.

"There's an extra dozen in the back," Hannah replied, then glanced at Lucy with a sly grin. "Are you thinking of bringing some to Taylor?"

Lucy felt her cheeks flush as she nodded. Taylor was the deputy sheriff in Ivy Creek and Lucy had recently begun dating him... again. They had once been high school sweethearts, but that had been a decade ago, and a lot of water had passed under the bridge since then. To say their relationship was complicated was an understatement.

The bell rang as someone entered the bakery, and Lucy turned to see who it was.

A young woman came forward, shyly saying hello. She carried a sheaf of papers and held one out to Lucy.

"Would you consider hanging this advertisement in your bakery?" she asked. "It's going to be a really fun Halloween attraction, and Mr. Marconi is hiring college students, like me, to play the monsters."

Lucy glanced down at the brightly colored flyer. *The Haunted Forest - A Hayride Full of Frights.*

"We sure will," she assured the young woman with a smile. "What a neat idea!" The girl thanked her, a pleased expression on her face as she left the bakery.

Betsy and Hannah crowded behind Lucy, reading over her shoulder.

Take a mile-long trip through the Haunted Forest, into the dark woods teeming with terror. You'll spot ghosts, goblins, and things that go bump in the night, guaranteed to make you shiver and scream. A Halloween adventure on a horse-drawn hay wagon, running Thursdays through Sundays in October. Come if you dare!

"Oh, how cool!" Hannah exclaimed. She looked at the address. "That's the old Sampson place. They have acres of woods out there."

Betsy commented, "That looks like a lot of fun! Joseph and I were talking about going to that haunted house attraction on the east side of town. What's it called?" Her brow furrowed.

"The House of Horrors?" Lucy asked. She'd heard the cashier talking about it at Bing's Grocery and wondered if it would be worth the admission price.

"Right!" Betsy snapped her fingers. "House of Horrors. But this actually looks more enjoyable, outside… under the moon…"

Hannah looked at the two of them, her eyes widening. "Hey, let's all go together! Kick off the spooky season with a bang. Or a Boo!" she joked. She looked over at Aunt Tricia. "What do you think, Tricia?"

Aunt Tricia smiled but shook her head. "I'll leave that sort of stuff to the younger crowd. But you girls should go."

Betsy ventured, "I bet Joseph and Taylor would go, don't you think?" She looked at Lucy.

Lucy smiled, amused by the notion of them all together on a spooky hayride. "I'm sure they would." She had a sudden thought and turned to Betsy. "That girl said they were hiring college students to play the monsters. Maybe you should mention it to Joseph's nephew, Derek."

Betsy nodded. "I was thinking the same thing. I'm sure he could use a few extra bucks. And it's acting… technically."

Hannah's face was filled with eager anticipation as she looked at her friends. "So, what do you guys think? Maybe Friday night?"

Lucy and Betsy exchanged glances and grinned.

"OK!"

"I'm in!"

"Excellent," Hannah proclaimed. She grabbed her apron off the hook, tying it around her waist. "This is going to be a blast!" She disappeared into the back to begin baking.

Lucy took the flyer to the front wall, tacking it up on the corkboard. She studied the colorful advertisement, smiling at the mental image of the five of them, *"kicking off the Halloween season with a Boo"*.

A night out in the crisp autumn air, under the moon, clinging to each other and squealing in mock horror. *A silly adventure*, she thought. *Lighthearted fun.*

She couldn't have been further off the mark.

DOUGH SHALL NOT MURDER

AN IVY CREEK COZY MYSTERY

RUTH BAKER

ALSO BY RUTH BAKER

The Ivy Creek Cozy Mystery Series

Which Pie Goes with Murder? (Book 1)

Twinkle, Twinkle, Deadly Sprinkles (Book 2)

Waffles and Scuffles (Book 3)

Silent Night, Unholy Bites (Book 4)

Waffles and Scuffles (Book 5)

Cookie Dough and Bruised Egos (Book 6)

A Sticky Toffee Catastrophe (Book 7)

Dough Shall Not Murder (Book 8)

NEWSLETTER SIGNUP

Want **FREE** COPIES OF FUTURE **CLEANTALES** BOOKS, FIRST NOTIFICATION OF NEW RELEASES, CONTESTS AND GIVEAWAYS?

GO TO THE LINK BELOW TO SIGN UP TO THE NEWSLETTER!

https://cleantales.com/newsletter/